"Don't start talking sex."

Gage's tone was pleading as he suffered a slow inexorable tightening of the nether regions of his body. "You have to learn that talking about it is erotic, at least to a man."

Phoebe sat back on her heels and demurely clasped her hands in her lap. "You mean if I just talked about what we did in the boat, without even touchin' you, you'd—"

"Exactly."

"Lor!" Unexpected streams of excitement lazily uncoiled inside her. "Gage? Did you like the part where I unbuttoned your shirt and—"

"I'm not listening."

"What about when I unzipped your pants—"

"Be quiet!"

"What about . . ." Phoebe put her lips to his ear and whispered.

With an unsteady arm Gage reached out and encircled her. "I'm lost," he groaned.

Jackie Weger was a little nervous when she began working on Phoebe's story. She and her husband, H.A., had just moved away from Texas, and Jackie was afraid she'd left her muse behind. With bated breath, we waited for *Eye of the Beholder*. Could Jackie still work her magic?

The answer was a resounding yes. Obviously, writer and inspiration have been happily reunited in Alabama.

Books by Jackie Weger

Don't miss any of our special offers. Write to us at the following address for information on our newest releases.

Harlequin Reader Service
901 Fuhrmann Blvd., P.O. Box 1397, Buffalo, NY 14240
Canadian address: P.O. Box 603,
Fort Erie, Ont. L2A 5X3

Eye of the Beholder

JACKIE WEGER

Harlequin Books

TORONTO • NEW YORK • LONDON
AMSTERDAM • PARIS • SYDNEY • HAMBURG
STOCKHOLM • ATHENS • TOKYO • MILAN

For my dad, Jack "Rabbit" Bolling,
former first baseman for the Brooklyn Dodgers
and a star in his own right.

Published December 1987

ISBN 0-373-25281-1

1

PHOEBE'S PACE HASTENED as she approached her truck parked in the lee of the building near the big trash compactor. She'd had to find a spot away from prying eyes because she couldn't trust Maydean and Willie-Boy to behave without her standing over them. Like now, she noted, discovering Willie-Boy hanging out the window.

"Did you get work?" he asked.

"Not yet," Phoebe said, brushing off the fact that the interviewer had insulted her down to muscle and bone. "I didn't want that old job nohow. Dern it, Maydean. I told you not to mess with that mirror, didn't I?"

Twelve-year-old Maydean flounced. It took her whole body to do it. "How much money we got left, Phoebe? I'm hungry."

Phoebe didn't want to think about money. Or buying food. Or where they were going to sleep that night. She reached up, adjusting the mirror. "We'll eat when I get hungry."

"You never get hungry! And you're never going to get no job, either. You're too skinny. I told you! If you want to work in the city you got to have a figure. I told you! Stuff toilet paper in your bra. There ain't nobody going to hire a flat-chested string bean like you. Not to work in no office, they ain't. And you oughta dyed your hair. Folks take one look at that fire-engine red and they know right off you got a temper. Know right off you're skinny and mean. You ain't never going to find us a place, Phoebe. I know you ain't. Ma should never have trusted you to do it. We'll probably never see Ma and Pa and Erlene the rest of our lives."

For an instant Phoebe closed her eyes against the bright glare of the sun. Pride and anger warred within her. In her heart she wanted to be as good and kind thinking as the all-forgiving Lord meant her to be. But right this minute she felt awfully like grabbing a handful of Maydean's hair. "I wish I had your cold heart, Maydean. Then I wouldn't be worryin' about what to do next, where our next meal is comin' from or where we're gonna sleep tonight. Anyhow, it ain't in the chest. It's in the backbone. Hair color don't make no nevermind. Now shut up. You're makin' me mad. Hike up and look out over that trash bin. I got to back out." She focused on her sister with an expression so fierce Maydean grudged a skittering glance over her shoulder.

"Nothin's comin'."

But there was, and Phoebe backed right into it. A pickup, newer than her own, but not much newer. Still, she felt her mouth going uncommonly dry.

"We're goin' to jail now, ain't we?" cried Willie-Boy. He scrambled to his knees to look out the cracked back window. "Lor, Phoebe," he whispered. "There's a giant gettin' outen that truck."

Phoebe watched the man emerge. Labeling him giant wasn't far wrong. Tall and broad-shouldered, he had a waist tapering into well-cut jeans filled out so she could tell he had never missed a meal. She left off watching him disentangle his legs to focus on his face. He was putting on a frown.

The eyes were dark, deep set and thick lashed. Sparking eyes, Phoebe thought. Most likely he used them to advantage on women. The idea made her feel an odd fluttering in her stomach. Had she been able to snag a man like him back home, why her whole family would still be together.

The rest of the man's face was filled out with a good straight nose and kissing lips. All over his head was curly black hair, tidily cut. Went to the barbershop every month most likely. Curls like that couldn't be kept aright if left to grow wild. She ought to know. It'd been months since she'd had her own curls parlor cut, and now they slipped band and pin and pomade with fierce regularity.

The man was looking at her. Phoebe saw the kissing lips turning down at the corners and the good straight nose beginning to narrow like he was smelling dead fish. Edgewise she caught a glimpse of Maydean patting her hair and puckering her lips, one hand on the door handle. Phoebe grabbed her.

"Stay put," she ordered. "You too, Willie-Boy. I'll see how much damage he done." Adjusting her cotton skirt and brushing trailing wisps of red hair back from her face, Phoebe stepped out of the truck. "How 'do," she said, politelike. She tracked all of him in a close-up glance before she gave her attention to their locked bumpers. "Looks like you hit me a fair blow, don't it?"

His gaze darted over her, taking in the narrow, heart-shaped face, the shoulders, true and squared, slender legs below the flowered skirt, the once-white sneakers, laces knotted twice over where they'd broken. His eyes lifted back to her face where wisps of red hair— hundreds of them—were all astray. Phoebe watched the frown spread out all over his face. He hadn't answered her and she was not equipped to meet silence. She spoke again.

"I said—"

"I know what you said. It's the other way round. You ought to look where you're going."

Phoebe tried not to pay attention to his voice. It was deep, good sounding and smooth. "I was looking," she said resolutely. "I didn't see you."

"I came out of that parking space." He waved his hand in an easterly direction. It was a big hand, finely shaped and callused. The calluses impressed Phoebe. A woman couldn't go much wrong latching onto a man with calluses. It took steady work to thicken skin like that.

Phoebe decided to be friendly, generous of spirit. She was proud of her teeth. They were white and even with no gaps. She gave him her best smile. "I can't tell which dent I did you or you did me. We can call it even, I reckon."

"Even?" He eyed her with suspicion. "Are you telling me you don't have any insurance or money to make good on the damage you did my truck?"

All sorts of dreadful apprehensions began to rise in Phoebe. Still, she was reluctant to give up being friendly. "I'm not sayin' any such thing. I don't discuss personal things like that with strangers."

He muttered something beneath his breath. "I didn't catch that," Phoebe said, hanging on to her smile.

"You probably don't have a driver's license either. You old enough to drive?"

Offended, Phoebe bristled. Her smile faded. "Way old enough."

"How old?"

"Twenty-six."

Disbelief made his eyes go cloudy. "I'm going to call the cops."

"Twenty-five. Almost. I swear. That's what it says on my license." The truth was that she was twenty-four, looking to be twenty-five and an old maid. She wanted to skip being twenty-five. She decided against any further friendliness. "'Scuse me a minute." She sidled up to the cab where Willie-Boy and Maydean were arguing for gawking space. "Count to ten, Maydean, then you two start wailing."

Wearing her most serious expression she rejoined the man. He was scowling at the locked bumpers. "If you stood on yours," she suggested, "big as you are, I could drive my truck right off it."

"One of us is bound to lose a bumper."

The caterwauling began. He looked up startled. "What in hell—"

"When you run into us, they hit their heads on the windshield. Like I said, you hit us a fair blow."

His whole body went rigid as a block of granite. "I didn't run into you, lady. You backed into me."

"My sister and little brother said you run into us. They were watchin'."

"And that's what you'd tell the cops," he replied, sarcasm flowing.

"Well, not me, mister. I didn't see you and that's a fact. But Maydean did, certain." Phoebe aimed an anxious look toward the noise. "We better figure somethin' out quick. I might have to take those kids to the hospital."

He growled an epithet. Ladylike, Phoebe pretended not to hear. Her eyes stayed glued to his face. He was making a decision, she could see it in his expression.

"A fender bender's not worth the trouble," he said. "I'll stand on the bumper, you see if you can pull your heap off."

Moving quicker than a sprite, Phoebe got back in her truck. "Y'all can quit your snivelin' now."

"I can't," whimpered Willie-Boy. "Maydean pinched me."

Phoebe hung her head out the window. "Hey, mister, you set?"

"I'm set." He gave a tentative bounce on the bumpers. "You go slow. Easy and slow. I don't want to end up with a broken leg."

Phoebe put the truck in forward gear while he rocked the bumpers. The vehicles parted with a screech. Her flesh crawled. It sounded worse than chalk gone awry on a blackboard. She got out and went to the rear of her truck again.

"Afraid your bumper came clean off," said the man.

"That's okay," said Phoebe. "I can weld it back once I get the chance. Just toss it in the back yonder, will you? On top of our suitcases and such."

Effortlessly, he picked up the torn and bent metal. Phoebe noticed his face didn't even go red with the strain. When he had the bumper chest level, his dark eyes held hers a heartbeat. Then he tossed the bumper into the bed of his own truck.

"Hey! Hey, mister, you can't do that. That's my bumper."

"Sure it is. And when you get the money to pay for the damage you did mine, you can have it back."

Phoebe's wide eyes narrowed to slits. "That's a mean trick, mister. I've got to have that bumper. It's got my tag on it. I can't go drivin' around Alabama with no tag. Troopers would stop me, sure."

He brushed his callused hands together. "I'll take good care of it for you. You just come out to G. G.

Morgan's junkyard when you get the money. It's on the other side of the bayou. Ask anybody to point the way."

Phoebe's heart sank. "C'mon, mister, can't we talk this over?"

"I'm done with talking, I'm late for an appointment." He stepped into his cab, slamming the door then leaned out over his elbow. "You're real slick, little lady, but you'll have to go some to outslick G. G. Morgan."

"I got seven dollars," Phoebe called with a failing heart. "You can have it."

G. G. Morgan lifted an eyebrow and laughed. "Come up with seventy and we'll do business."

Riding fury, hands balled into fists and propped on her hips, Phoebe watched G. G. Morgan maneuver out of the parking lot into light midmorning traffic. Watched her bumper and tag disappear. Her shoulders sagged, and for once her brain couldn't grab hold of any ideas. She felt tired. The worrying and the driving and the hope she'd been harboring—all of it hit her at once.

"You look fretted," Willie-Boy said when she slid onto the seat beside him.

"I got things to fret about, don't I?"

"We ain't goin' to sleep in the back of the truck again tonight, are we?" asked Maydean, puckering her lips into a peevish moue, which she thought most attractive. "I'm gettin' tired of that. I still got wrinkles in my skin from last night."

"You got wrinkles in your brain, Maydean. Be quiet and let me think."

"How're we gonna get our bumper back?" Willie-Boy wanted to know.

"I'm studyin' on it," Phoebe said, forcing up the determination not to let things get her down. That was Pa's problem. He let things carry him into a sulk so as nothing got done. Phoebe fought the feeling, afraid it was a family failing. She wasn't sure, but she thought that was what had happened to Erlene. Erlene had been fine until she went into a sulk with a fever. When the fever went, Erlene's grown-up mind had gone with it.

"What we'll do . . ." she said, shaking loose old thoughts, "is, we'll just go out to G. G. Morgan's junk-yard and get the bumper when he ain't lookin'."

Willie-Boy's eyes grew wide. "Ain't that stealin'? Ma said—"

"Stealin' is when you take something that don't belong to you. That bumper is ours."

"You shoulda let me handle it," said Maydean. "I have sultry eyes. Everybody in Cottontown says so. G. G. Morgan woulda looked into my eyes and I coulda made him give us our bumper. And, speaking of my eyes, Phoebe, first chance you get, buy me some mascara?"

Phoebe bit down on her tongue to keep from screaming. "Maydean, when you bat your lashes all you look is cross-eyed. Besides, G. G. Morgan didn't strike me as the swoonin' type. Now get out and watch traffic so I can back out. That is, if you can see anything besides pants with your sultry eyes."

Maydean sniffed. "You're just jealous cause my lashes are longer'n yours and I poke out more in front."

"Stand behind the truck, Maydean. Then I won't have to worry 'bout feedin' you."

"What pokes out?" asked Willie-Boy.

"Never you mind," Phoebe chastised, grinding the gears and backing safely away from the trash compactor. "We've got to find a telephone," she said when Maydean flounced back into the truck. "Y'all keep an eye out."

Willie-Boy jumped excitedly. "We gonna call some-body? We gonna call Ma?"

"No. I got to get an address on that junkyard."

"Lor, ain't you smart," Willie-Boy said with flatter-ing awe. "I'm goin' to be as smart as you when I grow up."

Phoebe drove a quarter mile and found herself out-side the small town. The road was narrow, lined on one side by ditches carved out of red clay and on the other by oak trees thick of trunk and gnarled landward by wind that swept in from the bay. "Goin' the wrong way," she said, whipping around in a U-turn. It wasn't lost on Phoebe that lately her whole life was filled with U-turns, leading her from nowhere back to nowhere. Well, she meant to change all that. Somehow.

"There's a cop followin' us," said Maydean.

Phoebe's gaze flew to the rearview mirror in time to see the red ball start flashing. "If it ain't one thing, it's ten," she moaned. She pulled onto the verge and shut the motor off, waiting.

"Howdy," said the trooper.

"Mornin'," replied Phoebe.

"Mind if I see your license?"

"No sir, don't mind a'tall." She dug around in her change purse and handed it out the window. "Nice day, ain't it?"

"Cottontown. You're a long way from home, aren't you, miss? Cottontown's north. What brings you to Bayou La Batre?" He ran the words together so that to Phoebe it sounded like Byabatrie.

"We're visitin'," she said, keeping to a vague truth.

"I see. It appears you're missing a license plate, though."

"It's on the bumper," Phoebe informed him.

"Is that right? Appears you're missing a bumper, too."

"Yessir. It fell off. This is an old truck. Bolts rusted. Darn thing just fell flat off."

The trooper thumbed her driver's license and stared into the truck. Phoebe tried to figure out what he was thinking. She knew they looked bedraggled and poor, which they were. But they were clean; she had seen to that at the rest stop earlier that morning. No doubt the trooper guessed that even if he gave her a ticket, she wouldn't have the money to pay it.

"Who're you visiting in Bayou La Batre?" he asked.

"What?"

"You said you were visiting. Who? Relatives?"

"Oh." Phoebe's thoughts flew. "Cousins. We're visitin' a cousin."

"This cousin have a name?"

Name? *Name!* Phoebe didn't know a soul in— "Morgan, G. G. Morgan."

The trooper's eyes narrowed. "Gage Morgan?"

Phoebe's heart did cartwheels. "That's him. Unless—how many G. G. Morgan's you got in Bayou La Batre?"

"Only one I know of is Gage. Never knew he had any cousins anywhere. Leastwise he never mentioned it and we went through school together."

"We're cousins three times removed, maybe more," said Phoebe. "But, ain't that something!" she gushed. "You and Gage bein' schoolmates all those years. Why…that makes you and me almost family friends." She pointed to her sister. "That there is Maydean and this is Willie-Boy, G. G. Morgan's least cousin. Truth is, we just ain't had time to visit afore now." Maydean's puckering lips fell open. Willie-Boy's, too. Phoebe crooked her elbow, jambing it under his chin to keep his mouth shut lest he contradict her.

"Gage has our bumper and tag in the back of his truck. He's waitin' on us, out to the junkyard so we can weld it back on." It was something, Phoebe thought, how a body could take a tidbit of truth and bracket it with lies and make it sound so good. Noting the trooper was swallowing it all, she gave her whole face up to a grand smile.

"Why didn't you say so in the first place? Tell you what. I'll follow you over to Gage's, else going back through town you get stopped again, no tag and all." He returned her driver's license.

Phoebe protested hardily. "Oh, we wouldn't want to put you out none." In her mind's eye she could see G. G. Morgan disputing all that she'd told the trooper. It wasn't a comforting thought.

"It's no trouble. The yard's barely a block out of my patrol area. Besides, it's part of my job to help folks."

"Then maybe it'd be better if you led the way."

The trooper squinted, suspicion flaring. "Why?"

"We just got into town this mornin'," Phoebe said. "We ain't been to the junkyard yet. When the bumper fell off, Gage came and got it. We were followin' him, but I got lost 'cause of Willie-Boy here, a-squirming something awful on account of a full bladder. . . ." She trailed off and closed her mouth. Casting her eyes down she held all the air in her lungs and pressed to make her face go red; mention of body functions and such never did have the effect of making her blush. She canted a furtive look at the officer. Her demure look and her flaming face were having the desired effect.

"Right," he said. "But, you stay close now."

Phoebe was torn between holding her breath and smiling at him. Need of air won. "Yessir." She pulled out behind the cruiser, sighing relief when the twirling red light went dark.

"We're in trouble sure," announced Maydean. "All them lies you told, Phoebe. That cop's gonna know soon's we get to the junkyard."

"You go to hell if you tell lies, Ma said," piped up Willie-Boy, gazing at Phoebe as if she would go up in flames any minute, or at least get hit by flying brimstone.

"We didn't get a ticket, did we?" Phoebe said, justifying her actions. "We're bein' led right to where our bumper and tag is, ain't we? Besides, everybody's brothers in the eyes of the Lord. Says so right in the Bible. If you have brothers, stands to reason, don't it, you got aunts and uncles and cousins?"

Maydean giggled. "Maybe us and G. G. Morgan are kissin' cousins."

Phoebe threw her sister a sharp glance. "You keep talkin' that way, Maydean, I'll slap you. And get your hair off the top of your head like that. You look like a worn-out tart."

The twelve-year-old sniffed. "You oughta see what yours looks like. Red hairs are crawling outa that knot atop your head so fast, they look like they're running from a cootie convention."

"I had cooties once, didn't I, Phoebe? Ma shaved my head and rubbed it down with kerosene. Burned somethin' fierce, I recall."

"Hush talkin' about lice, Willie-Boy. Help me keep that cruiser in view." Phoebe shot another glance at Maydean. If she'd had her druthers, she'd 've taken Erlene on this trip instead of Maydean, even if she did have to point Erlene in every direction she meant for her to go. Maydean was ripening too fast. Phoebe briefly thought about ways to hold back nature. But thinking on Maydean was just using up energy better spent elsewhere at the moment.

"We're goin' over the drawbridge again!" whooped Willie-Boy.

"Lookit the sailors on those boats," cooed Maydean. Suddenly she thrust half her body out of the truck, threw up her hands and waved.

Phoebe grabbed Maydean's blouse and yanked her back. "Another stunt like that and I'll put you on a bus back to Ma!"

Maydean smirked. "You ain't got the money for no bus ticket."

"I'd find the money," said Phoebe, her grinding tone so filled with resolution that Maydean appeared to believe her.

Driving past the building where she'd been refused work, Phoebe kept her eyes straight ahead of her. Another three blocks and the patrol car slowed, turning onto a sandy road that was little more than a well-used path, rutted and grooved by far heavier vehicles. In some places the road went right up to the bayou's edge, in others it zigzagged around boat yards and barge fitters and commercial net shops. Green and black nets sagged like larger-than-life spiderwebs from booms jutting thirty feet into the salty air. Far back on the landward side were seafood houses where signs advertised that crabs were boiled and picked, shrimp was packed, oysters were shucked.

Phoebe eyed the seafood packagers with interest; the possibility that she might find work in one of them filled her with hope. Mayhap losing her bumper wasn't such a bad thing after all. She never would've thought to drive down such an unpromising-looking back road.

"The cop's a turnin' in," Willie-Boy said excitedly. "Phoebe," he gasped. "Lookit! Lookit all that good stuff. I see a bicycle. It ain't got no wheels, but you could put some on it. Then I'd have me a bike. I allus wanted a bike."

"I can't study a bike right now. I'm lookin' for G. G. Morgan or his truck." Phoebe set the brake, but didn't shut off the motor. She gazed at the acres and acres of wrecked cars, boat ribs, tires and shapeless metal. "Piled up on good ground," she muttered. "Why a man could clean all that trash off and plant a fair good crop of cotton or corn and make something of himself. Why, even me and Ma could make a go, had we land—" She caught herself prattling and clamped her lips closed. She had no call to talk like that—or dream, either. Not while she was square on property that belonged to a man as unlikely to share it as G. G. Morgan. *Do first what first needs doin'*, she told herself. *Get rid of the police.*

Maydean opened her door. Willie-Boy scrambled over her and leaped from the truck. "Get back here," Phoebe demanded. "Maydean, you let him out on purpose!"

"He said he had to go to the bathroom."

"My foot! His nose is twitchin' to explore worse'n a blue tick hound. Get after him. In this heat he's liable to come down with an attack of asthma, and I ain't got the time to fool with—"

"He don't like me pryin' when he's takin' a leak."

The officer ambled her way. "Looks like Gage hasn't got here yet," he said.

"No doubt he missed us behind him and doubled back. Sure as anything he did. He warned me to keep close. We sure are bein' a peck of trouble. But now Gage'll be mad enough to throw us out on our ear," she said, in case he appeared suddenly and did just that.

The radio in the patrol car began to crackle. The officer excused himself. "You'll be okay now you're here," he said upon his return. "I've got to work an accident. You tell Gage I said hello."

"That'll be the first thing I tell him," agreed Phoebe. If she ever saw him again, which she hoped she didn't. "You be careful, you hear," she called to the trooper. "And, thanks." She forced herself to sit still until the cruiser was out of sight. Then she had to spend a precious ten minutes locating her siblings.

Maydean had found herself an old car with a mirror intact. Willie-Boy was sitting behind the wheel pretending he was a race car driver. They were frittering away time—carefree, without a thought in their heads as to how they were going to get decently sheltered and raised. No, they left that suffering to her, thought Phoebe. But the kids weren't visible unless someone was to peer directly into the old car so Phoebe decided they'd be out of harm's way for the few minutes she needed to scout the junkyard.

She began looking for a place to park. A shady place and one that was not directly in view of anyone driving through the old gate. There was no sense alerting the junkyard's owner that they were anywhere close by. At least not right off. If she found that there was no hope of reclaiming her bumper without Gage Morgan's interference, surprise made negotiating easier. And one way or another, Phoebe meant to be one whale of a surprise to G. G. Morgan. Most probably he wasn't a man used to having folks camp on his door-step until they got what they wanted. With all that was at stake, Phoebe figured she could outcamp and out-smart a truculent army of Huns. Gage Morgan was about to learn just how stalwart a Hawley could be.

2

PHOEBE AIMED THE TRUCK toward the rear of the yard. It looked to her as if G. G. Morgan lived smack-dab in the middle of his junk. Only the area around the weathered house was clear of rubble. Clear of saleable rubble that was, for the untended oasis was overgrown with chickweed, cat's ears and beggar's ticks. Shading the whole of it was a gnarled old tallow tree.

She eyed the house and unkempt yard behind the ragged wooden fence with strong disapproval. It was a sin the way some folks let things go down like that. Even the tallow tree looked dusty and beaten. Some folks, Phoebe thought, were just downright unappreciative of what the good Lord bestowed on them.

Unbidden, envy and resentment swelled within Phoebe. Why, if she had a house like that . . . if she had a square yard for flowers and vegetables . . . if she had land . . . she could send for Ma and Pa and Erlene, get them out from under her brother Joey and his new wife, Vinnie. What with only a four-room house, Vinnie didn't like the crowded conditions. She wore a permanent frown to prove it. Atop all that Vinnie was mean to Erlene. It wasn't Erlene's fault that she was loose-minded.

The truck hit a deep rut. Phoebe let go the wishful thinking and put her mind back on her present predicament. She needed to hide the truck and find a vantage point from which to spy on G. G. Morgan. The instant he left his truck untended she meant to retrieve her bumper and be gone.

She found a number of sheds and lean-tos, one of which was tilting precariously beyond the bulwark that held back a twisting saltwater canal. Beyond the canal, on the other side was the bayou that fed into the great expanse of the bay.

Phoebe's gaze went to the bay and farther, to the horizon. She had never seen the ocean. She had lived all her life in the foothills of the Appalachian Mountains where cotton and corn fields backed up to thick evergreen forests made dark and mysterious by creeping kudzu vines that could encroach on a garden or climb a sixty-foot pine—and do it overnight, some old-timers swore. Not a speck of kudzu hereabouts, Phoebe noted. That'd make Ma happy.

She backed the truck between two of the sheds, wedging in as far as she dared. Getting out of the driver's seat, she wiped the sweat beads from her nose and forehead with a quick duck of her head in the crook of her bent arm. The wind blew, cooling her more. She sniffed, inhaling the rich smell of warm earth and salt air, liking it.

As she retraced her path on foot, she noted a coop, disused, the gate hanging. Lor! But she could see hens nesting, eggs being gathered. Tomatoes and turnips sprouting where weeds grew. That one man owned so much—and did so little with it—was beyond comprehension. It was unholy.

"What're you doing out there?"

Phoebe froze. Her eyes darted, looking for the source of the voice. There came a squeak of unoiled hinges. She looked to the back of the house and saw a child standing just inside the screened door. Phoebe approached the back porch. She didn't know why, but she never expected the junkyard owner to have relations. More specifically she didn't expect a wife or child. A stab of disappointment caused the image of sparking eyes and callused hands to flit through her mind. She should've suspected it, most hardworking men had already been spoken for.

"I'm lookin' for G. G. Morgan," she said to the girl.

"He's not here."

The child, Phoebe could tell as she got closer, was about nine. She had an abundance of brown hair that needed brushing and a dirt-streaked, sunburned face that needed scrubbing. Altogether the girl looked as unkempt as the yard. Phoebe couldn't countenance a straight-minded woman letting yard and house and child lag so. Even Erlene, as cloudy-minded as she was, could do better.

"Is your ma here, then?" she asked.

The eyes, thick-lashed as G. G. Morgan's, became apprehensive. "No. She's gone."

"Where to?"

"Heaven."

"Oh." That explained it. Child, yard and house didn't have a woman's touch. Logic carried Phoebe to the thought that neither did the man. Disappointment fled. Opportunity raised its head and looked Phoebe square in the face. Stepping onto the porch, she chased away logic before it had a chance to gel. The kitchen was visible through the screen. Dirty dishes were on the table, piled on the sink. Dust, so old it had lost its color, lay on every surface from windowsill to chair backs. Hungering for things she didn't have, Phoebe itched to take up scrub brush and mop, just to have the feel of the familiar in her hands.

The child was staring at her, Phoebe plumbed her mind for what to do or say. "Is G. G. Morgan your pa, then?"

The girl nodded. "You're not supposed to be in the backyard. You want something you have to pay for it around front."

"I was just on my way." She couldn't keep from asking, "Who tends to you when your pa ain't here?"

The child's eyes shifted, the brooding stare becoming an angry glower. "I take care of myself. I don't need nobody. Mind your own business."

Phoebe bristled. "You need boxin' on the ears to teach you manners. It ain't polite to talk to your elders that way."

"You're not my elder. You look like a ragpicker."

Phoebe gathered all five feet of herself into one proud and stiff frame. "That's what I done all my working life until the mills shut down. When I see your pa, first thing I'm gonna tell him is that your tongue needs a set-to with Octagon soap." She spun off the porch and went to locate Maydean and Willie-Boy. For certain she didn't want them connecting with G. G. Morgan's girl. Maydean and Willie-Boy were ornery enough without learning new ways to go about it.

Maydean was still at the mirror, trying out different ways to pucker lips and flutter lashes. "Where's Willie-Boy?" Phoebe asked.

"Droolin' over that bike."

"He ain't. Maydean, I told you to watch your brother. Get outta there and help me look. No tellin' what pile of junk he's hidin' behind or climbin' about."

"It's too hot to go huntin' him up. I'm thirsty."

"Dead people don't thirst, Maydean. And that's what you're gonna be if you don't crawl outta that wreck and help me find Willie-Boy. I don't want us in sight when Gage Morgan trots back here. I aim to slip our bumper and ride out like lightnin'."

"A mule walkin' backwards can go faster than our old truck. He'll catch us."

"It won't do him any good. I aim to tape our license tag to the inside back window. If he catches up to us, we'll just roll our windows up and outwait him. One thing I figure Gage Morgan don't have is patience."

She called out for her brother, but met only silence.

"He's prob'ly playin' hide 'n' seek," suggested May-dean.

"If he is, he'll have to seek a new hide when I get done with him." Phoebe's own patience was wearing thin. She didn't like Willie-Boy being out of her sight. The junkyard was rife with paths going every whichway around heaps of old tires, wrecked cars and boats. All of which must look adventurous to a five-year-old with the urge to explore.

To Phoebe every pile of rubble held danger. Willie-Boy could be suffocating under a mountain of old tires, lying broken beneath a slide of metal, dead in high weeds, snakebit. With a queasy feeling in the pit of her stomach, she sent Maydean one way; she went an-other.

She couldn't help thinking that it had all been too easy. Outside of G. G. Morgan setting his sights on her bumper, being led straight here by the police when he could've just as easily given her a ticket, finding a good place to hide the truck . . . *Things just don't go easy for people,* she said to herself. *Something's bound to come and spoil it.*

"Knew it!" she muttered when she found Willie-Boy draped over the prow of an old wooden boat on the bank of the canal. He was suffering an attack of asthma and gasping for air. "It . . . come . . . on me . . . sudden," he rasped.

Phoebe's spirit sagged. She was running out of money, hadn't found a job, hadn't found a house and she had two kids in hand to feed. One of whom had now gone and got sick. *If the Lord is watching over me, where's my share of help?* she wondered, feeling a stab of pity for herself. But she felt sorrier for Willie-Boy. Asthma was a beast, a hungry beast, and it sapped his strength, took away his good times, kept him sitting up at night, kept him housed when he'd rather be playing, seeing to little-boy junkets and adventures. The attacks scared him. He always thought he was going to die.

"I'm going to pick you up, Willie-Boy," she crooned. He hardly weighed more than a tubful of wet washing. "There's a nice shady porch out back of that house yonder. Soon's we get out outta this hot old sun, you'll be fine."

Maydean's path had led her back to the old car. Anxious to practice puckering again no doubt, Phoebe thought. Willie-Boy's gasping was getting worse. She yelled at Maydean. "Don't you even think once of climbin' back in that wreck, Maydean Hawley! Get round here where I parked the truck and get the inhaler. Willie-Boy's havin' an attack."

Phoebe put Willie-Boy on the back porch, propping him against one of the supports. The terrible sucking sounds he made trying to draw in oxygen made her wince. His face was red and sweat was pouring off him. Hesitantly, the girl came out of the house and stood beside Phoebe. Interest had replaced her sullen expression.

"What're you doing? What's wrong with him? You're not supposed to be back here."

"I need a bowl of ice and a rag," Phoebe told her. "A clean rag," she added recalling the state of the kitchen.

"My daddy won't like—"

Phoebe glared at the child. "You get me a bowl of ice and a clean rag. What your daddy might not like is my brother dyin' right here on his back porch. Quick now," she said more gently when the child's eyes flared with fear. Maydean brought the inhaler. Phoebe shoved it in Willie-Boy's mouth. It took him a half dozen good gasps to get the medication into his throat and down into his lungs. The terrible sucking sounds abated.

"What's your name?" Phoebe asked when the girl returned bearing ice cubes and a rag, gray and musty-smelling.

"Dorie Morgan."

"Well, you done good, Dorie Morgan." Phoebe began to wipe Willie-Boy down with rag-wrapped ice. When he began to take interest in his surroundings, when she saw his gaze go curiously to the girl, she handed him the rag and told him to keep at it himself.

"I almost died, didn't I Phoebe?"

"You didn't even come close. But when I whollop you for running and scampering in the sun like that, you're gonna wisht you hadda died."

"What the hell's going on here?" G. G. Morgan came out the screened door letting it slam behind him.

Phoebe's heart sank. All her advantage lost. She stood tall and glowered at him, sloe-eyed.

"You said to meet you here to get my bumper back. I'm here."

The junkyard owner looked at his daughter, at Maydean, at Willie-Boy before settling once again on Phoebe. "You turned up seventy dollars that quick?"

"Ain't turned up nothin' but here."

"This is private property. When you get the money, come to the front. That shed by the gate."

"Can't," said Phoebe, latching onto a blameworthy reason to give her some leverage. "When you hit us that lick this morning the excitement made Willie-Boy come down with a spell of asthma. After we got here, like you told us to, invited us practically, he knocked himself out on a piece of your junk. He can't be moved unless it's to a hospital. Reckon you want to pay the hospital bill?"

"Pay! Lady, I'm not paying for a damn thing. Your careless driving caused that wreck. And there's a sign on the gate that I'm not responsible for accidents."

"A sign don't mean nothing except that you know your property ain't safe. Willie-Boy's the proof of that I reckon. Anyhow. It's your word against mine. And the word of a Hawley is as good as you can get. You want to call it even and give me back my bumper, we'll just be on our way."

Gage was aware that he didn't know a lot about handling women or children. It seemed to him that the caustic-tongued redhead didn't fit either category. She was too old to be a child and, in his book, too rail-thin to be called a woman. What he did know was the bottom line. He spoke it. "Seventy dollars or no bumper."

"Ain't got seventy dollars."

Phoebe watched his mouth get thin-lipped. The thinner it got, the deeper became the frown between his eyes. The frown didn't hurt his looks any. But now wasn't the time to study on the man's looks. Still, her eyes strayed to the laundry-made creases in his shirt, his tanned, muscled arms, the balled fists propped at his belt line. She had the notion that a virtuous woman never stared at a man below the waist, so she dragged her eyes back to his face.

"You'll have to leave," said Gage. "When you get the money to repair my truck, you can have your bumper."

Phoebe heard him, glared at him and thrust her chin out. She knew the set of her jaw didn't make her look her best; Ma always said a body could set a nickel on her chin when Phoebe's dander was up. Well, her dander was up. She could feel bile racing through her veins. And she aimed to stay mad. When a woman got mad, a woman could get anything she wanted—if she just had the gumption to stay mad and not let up.

Phoebe believed she had so much gumption at the moment it threatened to spurt out her ears.

"You got a phone I can borrow? I want to call an ambulance for Willie-Boy, seein' as how I ain't got no bumper or tag, I can't drive him there myself. Seein' as how you ain't got the heart to let him recover afore you run us off. I imagine the folks at the hospital'll want to know how he come to be so bad off. Don't think I won't tell them. How you run into us, how you wasn't concerned about nothin' but your old truck and gettin' money outta poor folks."

Maydean started to cry. "I want to get outta here, Phoebe. We're gonna be in big trouble. We could go to jail. Welfare'll get us and separate us. You know what Ma said—"

"Go sit in the truck until you can get your wits about you, Maydean. This minute!" Maydean shuffled a few backward steps, refusing to budge farther.

"You're trying to lay a scam on me," said Gage Morgan. "It's not going to happen. People like you are always sniffing around for a hand-out. You came to the wrong place this time."

Phoebe skewered him with her see-all look, pondering the quality of G. G. Morgan, trusting to her backwoods instinct. Stubborn and tight-fisted, she figured. One thing she knew about a tight-fisted man: he craved an image of being generous in spirit while keeping his purse strings double-knotted. The mill owner back home had been exactly the same way, oozing nice words to Ma's face, when behind her back he was asking the sheriff to evict them. That picture recalled, Phoebe carried on, all acting fury.

"Since the beginnin' of time, a Hawley never accepted no charity. We always give fair value for anything we get. So you can just take back what you said about us grovelin' for a handout. It appears to me that you're so used to sellin' junk you think you can grab what belongs to other folks and sell it back. You think—"

"I'm going to throw up," said Willie-Boy.

Phoebe let up on G. G. Morgan. She tucked her skirt between her legs and knelt down beside her brother, holding his head over the side of the porch. Glancing slyly at the junkyard owner over her shoulder she watched his face go pale. It was something, she thought, how a man could bear up under a show of blood and fair faint at the sound of a dab of gagging. One thing she knew certain. She aimed to perch right here until Willie-Boy got better and she got her bumper back.

"If you're not up to paying the hospital for Willie-Boy, I reckon I can nurse him like I always done," she said. "That is, if you got a quiet place I can lay him down." She wiped Willie-Boy's mouth, then picked him up. His head lolled weakly against her shoulder, his legs draped over her arm, twitching. Expressions were fleeing across Gage Morgan's face. Phoebe could see him deciding about a sure thing—in favor of his purse.

"How long will it take him to recover?"

Phoebe thought: *Until I find a job and make seventy dollars.* "An hour, maybe two," she said.

Scowling, Gage opened the screened door and waved her through. Sharp-eyed, Phoebe took in the kitchen, the wide central hall beyond, the doors leading off it. "Where can I put him?" she asked.

Gage pointed. Phoebe went. It was a cramped and musty little room with spider webs draped and barely hanging on in the corners. It had a dresser and a double bed with the mattress rolled up exposing old iron springs. The dust was terrible, not at all good for Willie-Boy. The room's only redeeming feature was the butter-yellow sunshine shining through the window. Phoebe called to Maydean.

"Lay out that mattress."

"You reckon it has bedbugs?"

Phoebe shot a look behind her but Gage Morgan was gone, in his place stood his daughter. "Don't look a gift horse in the mouth, Maydean." She lay Willie-Boy down on the bare ticking, stretching his legs out. To Dorie she said, "You want to show me where you keep a bucket and soap? And a sheet?"

"What're you going to do?"

"Clean this room. If I don't, Willie-Boy won't get well."

"This was my mama's room."

Phoebe's pale brows shot up. "Your pa's, too?"

"No, just my mama's. She didn't like my daddy."

"Marriage can be a terrible trial if you ain't married to the right person," Phoebe agreed.

"Mama liked me, though."

"You miss her, don't you? It's a sad thing when a mother is taken up and leaves younguns behind." She followed Dorie into the kitchen. The child pointed out the pantry.

"If Mama had taken me with her that day, she wouldn't've drowned. I can swim real good. I could've saved her."

"I'll just bet you could've."

Phoebe didn't know where all this was leading. That the girl was troubled was plain. Later she could worry on the child. Just now, getting settled was the main thing. She looked up at the ceiling. Lor, but having a roof above one's head was a precious thing.

From somewhere at the other end of the rambling old house, Gage Morgan called for his daughter. Before the child went to answer his summons, Phoebe saw the way Dorie's face tightened. A hornet's nest, that's what she'd stepped into, Phoebe thought. Digging around in the pantry for the things she needed, she amended the thought. Dern *dirty* hornet's nest! She put her hand around the mop handle and sighed happily.

STANDING AT THE FOOT of the bed Phoebe turned slowly and admired her work. The small room gleamed clean and cheerful. Not even a vagrant dust mote hung in the air for the sun to illuminate. Maydean was polishing the mirror on the dresser with newspaper and vinegar. What with Maydean's love affair with her mirror image, Phoebe figured that'd keep the twelve-year-old content and out of harm's way for an hour or two. What was pressing down on Phoebe now was hunger.

She could feel the pangs, stabbing and fixing to get noisy.

"I feel good now, Phoebe," said Willie-Boy from the bed. He was lying on a clean pink sheet and propped up on a pillow they'd discovered in the closet. "I can get up now."

Phoebe was thinking hard. Everything she had in mind—survival, for today anyway—depended upon Willie-Boy being ill. And staying that way. Looking at the five-year-old, she struggled with her conscience. She had to decide between Hawley scruples and dire need. Need won out. She sat on the bed and touched Willie-Boy's forehead. "You're not better yet, Willie-Boy. I can see it in your eyes."

"You can?"

"Sure I can. You know anybody with better eyesight than me?" She put her face right up to Willie-Boy's. "I can look into your eyes and see everything that's going on inside you."

He squeezed his eyes closed. "Don't look inside me, Phoebe. I got secrets. You're not supposed to know secrets."

"I have to look inside you so I know when you're well. But when I'm looking you can put your hand over your heart. That way I won't come upon anything you got to hide."

"You're sure?" Childish skepticism layered each word.

"Course I'm sure. You put your hand over your heart and it makes a dark shadow in there. You know how hard it is to see into shadows."

"Lemme get up, Phoebe. I feel okay. My chest don't hurt none."

"That's because it's numb. When the feelin' comes back I reckon I'll have to sit up with you all night."

"Here?"

"Right here in this room. Would you like that?"

"I like layin' on a mattress. It's softer than the back of the truck. But what about Mister Morgan?"

"I'll handle him," Phoebe said, wondering how. One thing was certain. Every word spoken to the man had to count. She suspected Gage Morgan had a fair amount of sense. Her idea was to not let him catch on that she knew it. With a word of caution to Maydean not to leave the room, she went to find the man who was her reluctant host.

The hall was wide, high and dim, the windows at each end so fogged with grime little light found its way inside. Of the six doors along its length one was slightly open. Phoebe peeked in. The bathroom. It needed a good scrub down. Another door was gaping. Dorie lay upon an unmade bed, coloring. Phoebe stood on the threshold.

"Where's your pa?"

Scowling, the girl looked up. "Out to the shed."

"What shed?"

"The welding shed. He fixes boat motors, propellers."

"Where is it?"

Dorie raised up and pointed out a window hung with once-white curtains gone gray and limp. "It's on the other side of the junkyard, facing the canal." Her eyes stayed hard on Phoebe for a few seconds then returned to the coloring book.

Phoebe ignored the child's dismissal. "How long's your ma been in heaven?"

The narrow face went dark. "Since last summer."

"Who does the cooking and cleaning for you and your pa?"

"Daddy does it."

Thinking on the state of the kitchen, Phoebe thought *No he don't*. Ideas raced so rampant in her head she was out the back door and across the junkyard before she had any good speaking words fixed solidly in her brain.

3

THE WELDING SHED was a great barn of a building constructed of metal. It was open at both ends so that standing at the landward end Phoebe could look straight through to the canal bathed in the sky's yellow haze. She slipped inside the yawning opening and stood there, giving her eyes the moments needed to adjust.

Propellers, large and small, lined the walls or hung suspended from ceiling beams on pulleys and chains—chains as thick as Gage Morgan's biceps. Phoebe could make the comparison because he was working on a propeller hung from just such a chain. He'd changed from his laundry-creased clothes into oil-stained khakis and a shirt with the sleeves cut out. The muscles in his arms rippled as he bore down on a bolt with a wrench.

Watching him caused a good-feeling sensation to spread warmth inside her. Lor, but it was fine to see a man work! Leastways, she now knew the source of those calluses on his palms. They'd be fair scratchy on a woman's tender skin though. She paused on the thought and caught herself running her hands up her arms.

Her midsection began to actively protest its hunger. The borborygmus issuing from her lower regions caught her off guard. The growling quaked so in her ears she misplaced the words she'd rehearsed. She cleared her throat as loud as she could.

Gage Morgan spun around and she noted the expression he wore didn't come anywhere near being kindly.

"Don't ever come sneaking up on me like that!"

"I'm no sneak." Offended, Phoebe regretted her good thoughts and the admiring of his body. "It's what's in your mind that makes a sneak. If I was aimin' to be sly, I could've slipped in and been here hours afore you discovered me."

"I'll give it to you that you're a sly one," he said acidly. "What do you want now?"

Pride went racing up and down Phoebe's spine looking for a way out. Before it got loose and did damage she said, "I just came to tell you Willie-Boy is some better."

"You're clearing out?"

He sounded so much like he wanted her to that Phoebe had to bite back the urge to say yes. "Willie-Boy's not up to bein' moved yet. He's fair weak what with throwin' up his breakfast and all." She paused, waiting to see how much sympathy that elicited. None! All the calluses in the world couldn't make up for a hard heart in a man. The dark, tightly wound knot under her ribcage that harbored hope shrank painfully.

"I came to see if I could buy a can of beans off your shelf or a couple of those near-to-rotten potatoes in that bag in the pantry. I figured some soup'd give Willie-Boy back his strength." For good measure and to jolt his conscience, she added, "If it comes to having to take Willie-Boy over to the hospital I want to be able to say you done all you could for him."

Gage made a noise in his throat. His gall was rising. He could taste it. "There's some women who can drive a man to drink or worse," he said, his jaw muscles going so tight his words hung in his throat. "You're one of them. Sly-tongued, manipulative harridans like you ought to be tarred and hung up to dry. Know this: there's not a woman in the world that can best me. Not after all I been through with a woman. You can just quit trying."

Phoebe had a flash of clarity. He was telling on himself without knowing it. No doubt a woman had gotten to Gage Morgan where it hurt the most—his purse. She tossed her head, which had the effect of making her curls fly.

"I don't take to slurring on my person. God made me a woman. You got problems with that, you take it up with Him. You gonna sell me a potato or not? I got to get some food in Willie-Boy lest he goes to faintin' with weakness."

Gage's fist tightened on the wrench. He waved it in the direction of the house. "Take what you want from the pantry. And the potatoes aren't rotten. I just bought them."

"Just did?" oozed Phoebe, ignoring the easy manner in which he was flailing the heavy tool about. Calling her names like that was unjustified. She wasn't going to back down just because she had brains and the man didn't like that. She ought to leave well enough alone. She had what she came for, but gumption overrode her practicality. "Well, the market put one over on you, mister. Those potatoes are sproutin'."

"No one puts anything over on me," he reiterated.

Phoebe ducked her chin and shoved her hands into her skirt pockets. "I reckon they don't," she crooned so smoothly, the sarcasm didn't catch. "You appear to be about the smartest man I ever met." On the outside. On the inside, he appeared to own a lacking she couldn't put a name to—yet.

His pupils dilated. "I'm not giving over to flattery from the likes of you. Get your brother up and about and get off my property. The sooner the better."

"I aim to," Phoebe answered forcefully, lest he pick up on the idea she meant to plop down like an old-time squatter spying the unprotected edge of a fine stone-free meadow.

Her feet itched to move but she didn't want to turn her back and allow him to watch her leave the shed. She knew she didn't have a hip-swaying walk that men kept on about. She pretended interest in her surroundings, gazing about the shed, above her head, along the walls until she spotted the bumper lying against some machine parts. Her eyes narrowed.

Tracking her gaze, Gage was alert to the instant her eyes alighted on the bumper. It was in her face, the way her mind worked. "Don't even think it," he said. "When I'm not working in here, this shed is locked tighter than an unopened drum. You want that bumper you come up with some cash."

Phoebe knew it wasn't in her nature to give up the last word; she allowed it on purpose. Let Gage Morgan think what he wanted. If he was so loose-minded he couldn't see that returning her bumper would turn her out of his house, she wasn't about to disabuse him.

She filled up her face with belligerence to hide her elation and let him get a good glimpse of it before she turned and exited the shed. On the off chance that taking mincing steps was how a woman achieved the hip rolling men admired, Phoebe tried it. She stumbled over her own feet. Behind her, Gage Morgan snorted.

Picking herself up, she shot a comment over her shoulder. "A body could break her neck on the clutter you keep."

Gage grinned. Phoebe was taken aback. Lor! He looked wonderful when he smiled.

"The only clutter in your path is at the end of those sticks you walk on," he said.

Phoebe drew herself up so still and tall she gained two inches. Gutter-minded man, she thought, smile or no. Inspecting her legs like that. Just went to show what kind of woman Gage Morgan would hook up to, *if* he got the chance. Which no doubt he wouldn't, considering how insufferable he was. Aggravation and mean thoughts occupied her all the way across the junkyard to the house and into the pantry.

The potatoes were Idaho, the prettiest Phoebe had held in her hand in many a week. She took them to the sink and cleared out a place to peel them. Gage Morgan's words had stuck in her craw. If ever she'd met a man who needed undoing, he was it. He needed to be unlaced so severely that everything he was just spilled out at her feet. Not feet. She didn't want to think about feet. There were a few things besides hip rolling that could set a man to thinking right about a woman. One of them was the smell of good food cooking. No doubt she'd figure out others as opportunities arose.

A closer inspection of the pantry shelves revealed condensed milk, sugar, packets of yeast, corn meal, dried beans, crackers and all manner of canned goods. Phoebe frowned at all the manna. It was just sitting there getting dusty and going to sinful waste. For shame. A woman trying to live right in God's eye wouldn't tolerate such. Phoebe grouped together the makings of a rich thick soup, corn fritters and fried potato doughnuts. If a body looked on it right, she was undoing sin and waste. God was probably looking down on her right this minute and beaming His approval.

Once the potatoes were boiling and the sugar yeast rising, she called Maydean and ordered her to clean the bathroom.

"Do the mirror last, Maydean, lest it get a hold on you."

"I ain't in the mind to clean somebody else's house. How long we gonna stay here?"

Phoebe looked out the kitchen window and saw prosperity: Ma weeding bean and tomato plants that marched in neat rows down to the canal. She saw Erlene scattering corn to chickens, Pa in his rocking chair on the back porch.

In the real world she spied the top of Dorie Morgan's head just beneath the windowsill. The scamp was eavesdropping. At the behest of her own pa no doubt.

"Just until Willie-Boy's well enough to travel," she posed with studied casualness.

"He's almost that now," claimed Maydean.

Phoebe could've throttled her. "He's not. He's weaker than I've seen him in a month of Sundays. If I was to move him now it'd have to be to a hospital." She shoved a bucket and a can of cleanser at Maydean. "Get in that bathroom and make it shine." Louder, she said, "I wonder where that Dorie got off to? Like as not, bedridden as he is, Willie-Boy'd like some company." She turned away from the window and began to clear the table. The screened door squeaked. "Oh, there you be," Phoebe said. "I was just—"

"My daddy said to stay away from you."

"Why?"

Dorie shrugged. "He just said, is all."

"If you lived in Cottontown where we come from, you'd be proud to associate with a Hawley. We got the reputation for being law abidin' and church goin'. Howsomever, I don't want you to go against your pa's word. So you can just clear outta this kitchen. I got floors to scrub, dishes to wash and doughnuts to fry."

Dorie hesitated. "Are you cooking for me, too?"

"You and your pa, if he's so-minded." Which Phoebe reckoned he would be once he got a whiff of her crisp-fried doughnuts. A right-minded man appreciated a woman who could cook. Phoebe didn't hold with all the other things men appreciated, mostly because she knew she was so thinly endowed with any of them. If she ever found a man who could look beyond body parts she'd latch on to him so quick. . . .

"Daddy eats at the restaurant in town."

"What about you?"

"He brings me hamburgers. I like hamburgers."

"Maybe tomorrow I'll make you a hamburger," Phoebe said. "That is, if Willie-Boy don't recover well enough to travel by dinner time. Howsomever, there's one thing I don't tolerate. That's a dirty face at my table. Once Maydean's got that bathroom clean, you scrub up."

The child bristled. "That's our table, not yours. I can sit any way I want."

"You can sit at it. You can own it. But I won't put no fried doughnuts on it lessen the faces around it are scrubbed and hair's combed. That's my final word."

Dorie stalked out. Phoebe started to call her back, but stopped. She didn't know what more she could say, or how much saying she could get away with. Anyway, at the moment the refrigerator needed her attention. It was big and solid and a light flashed on when the door was opened.

On the first shelf were good-quality milk, butter, cheeses and jellies. The lower shelves were crammed with bits and bowls of food gone rock hard or growing things. Lor! But this house needed constant seeing to by a woman. Most especially it needed a fine upstanding, hard-working woman who had lots of patience, a strong back, nice teeth and a frugal outlook to match its owner's. Phoebe thought she had all of that and a good heart to boot.

She had more than a good heart. It was ready to be filled with love. Though she had no evidence to support the idea, Phoebe told herself the junkyard owner appeared to need seeing to as much as his house. The bold thought sent a tingling up her spine. Having a house, having a man to call her own, especially a man as powerful and worthy of admiration as Gage Morgan . . . She shook her head as if to clear it of such foolishness.

But her good heart went to pounding like a jackhammer, speeding so that she felt compelled to clutch her chest to slow it down. The idea of pairing up with Gage Morgan wouldn't go away. It entertained her until she went to rummage for a sick-bed tray and dished up soup and corn bread for Willie-Boy.

"ARE YOU GONNA make me stay in bed the rest of my life?"

"Nope," replied Phoebe. "After you eat you're gonna get a nice hot bath."

Willie-Boy made a face. "I don't feel dirty."

"You don't feel sick, either, but you are. Don't go stubborn on me, Willie-Boy. I'm gettin' enough of that from the Morgans."

"I wanna go fishin'. You said if we got anywheres near water I could go fishin'. There's water every which way here."

"Phoebe!"

"Maydean, don't come up yellin' in my ear like that."

"There's a color television in the living room. It works."

"I told you to clean the bathroom, not to go snoopin' into closets and such!" Phoebe was saving the prying and poaching of the house for herself. She could do it better. She didn't like Maydean breaking ground first.

"It ain't in no closet. It's sittin' on a table, big as life. Dorie turned it on. Can I sit with her?"

Phoebe debated silently. She wanted to view the rest of the house. Just a look-see for now. The place she wanted her imprint on first was the kitchen. If she got her aura set there, why it'd just naturally follow her into every other room. But she had to be delicate about it. If Maydean was in the living room, why it stood to reason, she'd have to look in on her there. To make sure Maydean wasn't getting into anything she shouldn't.

"If you can get Dorie to the kitchen table with her face washed and hair combed to eat some soup then I reckon the both of you can watch television."

"If I can't go fishin' I wanna watch TV," announced Willie-Boy.

"Maybe after a bit I'll carry you in there," Phoebe agreed.

"I can walk."

Her mouth drew down at the corners. "You can't. And that's a fact. You want to watch TV, I'll carry you."

Speaking of carrying reminded Phoebe of the suitcases still out in the truck. It might look alarming if she toted them all in at the same time. She'd have to condense to get toothbrushes, pajamas and fresh clothes into the house. She picked up the bed tray. "You just let that food go down good, Willie-Boy. A nap won't hurt you none. After that you can have a bath, fried doughnuts and TV."

"You promise?"

"No. It ain't our house. I can't promise nothin'. I'm just sayin'."

"If it was our house, would you promise?"

"If it was our house, I'd let Ma answer your everlastin' questions."

"I wish Ma was here. She loves me. I'm her best boy." His eyes got wet, his mouth began to quiver.

Homesick, Phoebe surmised. "I got an idea. While you're restin' you be thinkin' of somethin' to say to Ma. I'll write it in a letter. Now, I got things to do." Weighted with the tray and problems needing solving, Phoebe hurried back to the kitchen. Gage Morgan was standing at the stove, peering into the soup pot.

Lor! The good cooking smells worked faster than she'd anticipated. "You set to the table," she said, "I'll fix you a plate."

Gage lifted his eyes to her, his expression bland. "This made out of my rotten potatoes?"

Phoebe cleared her throat. "I cut the bad spots out. They weren't so bad as I first supposed."

"I do my eating in town," he informed her, seeming to peer beyond Phoebe as if she didn't exist.

Plans goin' awry! Phoebe knew no way a woman could get a man if he wouldn't set still. "Seems to me it'd be a fair waste of good money to pay for ready-cooked food in a restaurant when you got home fixin's in your own clean kitchen." She began setting the table with the dishes she'd washed. "Your daughter, Dorie, commented she liked doughnuts. I'm fryin' some up soon's the batter rises. It's the least I can do for her, you lettin' us stay here and all." Moving around the table, Phoebe kept him in a corner of her vision. "Which is your chair?" She went to the stove, dipped up a bowl of soup. "Where you want it? There's corn bread, too. In the oven, stayin' warm."

Gage stared at her with a catlike stillness about his lean, hard frame. Grudgingly, he admitted to himself that Phoebe was right. He'd waste both time and money going out to eat. Even so, the girl's insouciance was insupportable... on the other hand, he hadn't had a home-cooked meal in months.

Phoebe watched his mouth alter shape, losing its hard stern line as if to smile. She opened her mouth to speak, but Gage walked on through and out of the kitchen into the house proper. She put the bowl on the table. Dipping up another cup of soup, she stood at the sink sipping on it. The best she'd ever made, she thought, staring out the window. This time no mindscape of visions came to her. No pictures of Ma or Pa or Erlene. The best-tasting soup she'd ever made sank like lead into her stomach.

Chair legs scraping the linoleum intruded upon her thoughts, grated on her nerves. She turned to chastise Maydean who had the bad habit of yanking chairs about and had to bite her tongue to keep the words from flying out.

Gage Morgan had taken his place at the table and was pulling the brimming bowl of soup toward himself. His cap of dark curly hair had been wetted and combed, his hands washed. Phoebe approved. It showed he had respect for the cook. A body on the alert for such could do a lot with respect, she thought, reckoning her alertness to be greater than if she'd been anticipating the effects of a double dose of castor oil.

"You like corn bread?" she asked, speaking up to cover the sudden quaking of nerve endings that were stimulating excitement in parts of her best ignored.

"Sure do."

Phoebe sliced two generous pieces and put great dollops of butter on each. "Didn't know about tea," she said. "There's ice water or milk." He chose water. Once he was eating steadily, she left him alone. Most men didn't like to be bothered when eating. Pa was like that. He hated having to swallow fast so as to make room for words.

She checked the plumpness of the sweet dough and set grease to heating in an iron skillet, moving from sink to pantry to stove as if being in his kitchen was the most ordinary of things. She fried a test batch of doughnuts. When they were nicely browned she drained them on paper and sprinkled them with sugar. "Some folks aren't up to sweets directly they've eaten," she said. "Which is it with you?"

"I'll try one."

She placed several on a plate. Gage ate them every one. Phoebe was proud to bursting. She had to turn away lest he see the happiness overtaking her.

"You folks on welfare or what?" Gage asked.

Phoebe spun around. Her jaw dropped. "Welfare! I ain't. We ain't. And never will be. Hawleys don't take to charity. We're workers!" She felt like thumping him on his back to get the doughnuts up.

"Don't get riled," Gage said, feeling mellow on account of his full stomach. "I was just curious."

"That kind of curiosity ain't polite."

He arched a brow. "You're in my house. I don't know you from Johnny Appleseed. For all I know you could clean me out the minute my back's turned."

Phoebe puffed up. "I come from good Christian stock. We ain't never stole so much as a nickel. For people, you won't find none better than a Hawley." Her look dared him to counter the truth of that.

"Where exactly do you come from?"

"Cottontown. Up north."

"Where were you headed when we had the fender bender?"

"I was headed for work," Phoebe said adroitly. "Like as not the folks won't save my job now, seeing as how I've been held up."

"You can use the phone in the living room to call if you want to," Gage offered.

"Better not. It'd be long distance. Thank you for offering." She put another batch of dough to frying. "I could write 'em, though. If you got a stamp I could buy."

"There's some in my desk."

Phoebe didn't know where his desk was. But it seemed he was giving her rein and trust to hunt it up. "I set Maydean to cleanin' the bathroom. You mind if I sponge Willie-Boy off? I'm worried he'll take to gettin' feverish if I don't. And if you'll tell me where you keep your wash tub, I'll rinse out the sheets off the bed in the mornin'. Leave 'em fresh, like we found 'em."

Gage moved to the door. "There's a washer and dryer in the storeroom off the back porch."

"Washer and dryer? You mean electric?"

"Electric," he said, studying her hard for a moment.

Lor! Phoebe was thinking, dirt and all, the house was a treasure trove of good things. A color television, a refrigerator with a light, a no-work washing machine, a pantry filled with food. "God has sure been good to you," she said.

"I could debate that. You cook whatever you want for supper." He glanced around the kitchen. "Appreciate you cleaning up the mess."

From inside the screened door, Phoebe watched him step off the porch and onto the path to the welding shed. Cook whatever she wanted for supper! If she was the swooning type, she reckoned she'd've done it right then. She didn't know what time Gage Morgan figured on eating supper, but it was plain he meant for her to be in his house to cook it. And tight-fisted as he was, he had manners, thanking her like that. Of course, the way he inspected and commented on a woman's body was scandalous. But a woman of virtue could lift a man out of wicked thoughts. Like as not a woman of virtue could coax a man to keep all his thoughts above the neck. Phoebe counted herself among the most virtuous of women that God ever had a hand in creating. Absolutely. She had never once dropped her drawers for a man. Never would either, unless…well, she would never be so stupid as to thwart the course of true love.

She went onto the porch and stared up into the noonday sun until a kaleidoscope of colors blocked out true vision. Prudence, temperance and fortitude swelled within her. Being noble was doing God's work. certain, she thought. Ma would be so proud.

"Whatcha doing standing out in the sun like that, Phoebe? You know it makes your freckles pop out."

What with feeling so fine spirited, Phoebe didn't like being reminded of earthly flaws. "I was prayin' over your food, Maydean, so you won't choke to death. The way you gobble I figured I'd better get as close to God as I could." Dorie was on Maydean's heels. Her face and hands were clean, her hair brushed into some order. The smell of fried doughnuts worked wonders. "Dish up soup for yourself and Dorie. Afterward you wash dishes. Dorie can dry."

"I hate doin' dishes. I'm tryin' to let my fingernails grow."

"If you're worried about your nails, Maydean, I can pluck 'em out."

"I'm goin' to tell Ma how mean you been bein' to me." She thrust out her lower lip.

Phoebe eyed Dorie who was listening hard. She didn't want much mention of Ma and Pa and Erlene just yet. "We're G. G. Morgan's guests. Proper manners requires us to wash up," she admonished. "Do a nicely neat job of it and I won't make you help me with the washin'. You can watch TV with Dorie and Willie-Boy."

Maydean kept her pout, but moved to the stove. Satisfied, Phoebe went to inspect the washer and dryer.

THE LAUNDRY ROOM HAD its own dusty four-paned window. Daylight streaming through revealed a copper-colored washer with a matching dryer. Long-dirty clothes and linens were piled atop both machines. Phoebe tsk-tsked. Along the opposite wall was another chest of white enamel. A Sears and Roebuck freezer. Phoebe put her hand on it and closed her eyes. It was empty no doubt. She lifted the lid and felt a blast of cold air. She opened her eyes and looked. Full!

There were packages upon packages labeled floun-
der and steak, whole chickens with plump thighs and
breasts. Ground beef, stew meat, green peas, lima
beans, ice cream. Ice cream! Phoebe kept rummaging
and looking until her fingers were so cold she had to
blow on them for warmth. Lor! A body would never
go hungry in Gage Morgan's house. She discounted the
dire manner he had toward women. Her estimation of
him went up. Oh! This afternoon while clothes were
drying on the line she'd sit down and write home. Ma
had been beside herself fretting that she'd have to swallow dignity and go stand in line to ask for food stamps.
Phoebe could relieve her of that worry. She lifted out a
fat chicken to thaw for supper.

Energy high, Phoebe went to the truck and retrieved
the sack of trip-worn, dirty clothes. It took her some
minutes to sort out how the washer worked, but once
it was filled with hot water and detergent, she managed a steady stream out to the clothesline. She longed
to use the electric dryer, but prudence suggested sun
drying.

Before she washed a single Morgan garment she inspected it, taking care that it was washed according to
instructions. Those belonging to Gage Morgan had a
smell about them. Of scent. Phoebe put one of his shirts
to her nose and inhaled. She got wicked thoughts. Lor!
She plunged it into the water.

When all the clotheslines were filled she stood in the
shade on the porch and watched towels and sheets and
shirts billow in the summer salt-breeze. She had worn
a path in the high weeds to the lines. It was almost like
trailblazing. Like being a pioneer woman. She had so
many good feelings inside she felt weak.

She had hung one of her blouses tail to tail with a shirt belonging to Gage Morgan. In her mind it was an intimate coupling, linking their lives.

All in all, thought Phoebe, this was most likely the best day of her life.

GAGE DID NOT COME up to the house for supper, but worked in the welding shed long after dark. Phoebe bathed herself and Willie-Boy and sent him and May-dean to bed.

Dorie balked at mention of bed. Phoebe let her be. The child fell asleep on the sofa. When Gage came in, he carried his daughter to her room.

"You want me to help you get her into nightclothes?" Phoebe asked.

"No."

"I set aside a platter of chicken and biscuits and gravy in the oven for you. You want I should put it on the table?"

"I'll eat in a bit."

Phoebe hesitated. Best thing she could do, she thought, was take herself off to bed, too, lest they engage in a conversation regarding her leaving at first light in the morning. "G'night, then."

Gage nodded absently. His attention was focused on Dorie. He was only now learning how to be a father. Dorie's mother had held the child up to the world, to himself, as an achievement of her own. Dorie had adored her mother and Velma enjoyed the adoration to an unhealthy degree. She had kept Dorie for herself. Wrongly, to keep peace, he'd allowed it. Now Dorie suffered for it, and he didn't know how to stop her suffering.

He brushed a wisp of hair from her forehead. Her round tanned face was clean for a change. The Hawley woman's doing no doubt. He wondered how she'd managed it. Dorie wore her dirt like a badge of honor.

It was too soon to tell, but perhaps allowing the transients into his home wasn't such a bad thing. Even if it was only for a day or two, they might be a pleasant diversion for Dorie.

He turned on the fan, turned off the light and went to get his supper. Pleasant for him, too, he mused when he bit into the chicken. He was the worst cook in the world.

4

PHOEBE AWOKE in the thin light of morning. Maydean was curled into a ball at the foot of the bed. Willie-Boy lay on his back. She put her ear to his chest. No sound of wheezing. That was good—and bad. She'd have to figure out a way to stay, beyond his recovery. *Trust a little to the Lord*, she told herself.

She had clean jeans and blouse to wear today. In the bathroom she yanked a brush through her hair, taming it as best she could. A woman had to look her best at first light, Ma always said.

She tiptoed down the hall to Gage's bedroom. The door was closed. She put her ear to it.

"Looking for me?"

She spun about. He stood at the head of the hall, holding a cup, looking suspicious. Phoebe cast about for the right words. "I was just hopin' my stumblin' around didn't wake you. I get fair noisy in the mornin'."

"You didn't."

She brushed past him, ever aware of his great height and powerful body. He followed her into the kitchen. Coffee was made. Phoebe poured herself a cup, savoring the rich-perked taste of it. "Willie-Boy passed a fair to middlin' night," she said.

"I'm glad to hear it."

"I washed all the clothes I found in the laundry hamper. I put Dorie's in her room, left yours folded in the basket. You want me to put 'em away?"

"I can do that."

"You want me to fix you some breakfast?"

"Never eat in the morning."

Never stretch out your words, either, thought Phoebe, hunting up something to say so an awkward silence wouldn't fall between them. "I got that letter written," she advanced, reminded of the envelope addressed to her mother. "Left a quarter for the stamp on your desk. You reckon I can put your address on it, so's they can write me back . . . if there's work?"

"Meaning?"

"Meanin' I can pick it up, if one comes after—" She stopped, not allowing the words to cross her lips. "Those seafood houses down the road, are they hirin'? I reckon I could earn enough money outta one of them to pay you for the bumper. That way, if there's still a job for me, I can get on the road quick."

He looked at her over the rim of his cup. "You ever pick crabs or shuck oysters?"

"I can pick and shuck with the best of them," she answered. She had shucked corn and picked cotton many a Saturday to earn extra cash. To her way of thinking picking crabs and shucking oysters couldn't be much different. She had never seen a live crab or oyster in her life, but she'd seen pictures in *National Geographic* in the library back home. She wasn't going to be outdone by any critter smaller than herself. Or bigger, she thought, eyeing Gage. "My hands are agile. My old boss in the cotton mills said I had the best hands he ever saw for threadin' bobbins."

"Threading bobbins?"

"That's right." Phoebe displayed her hands, thrusting them out, turning them over. "I know they appear waiflike, but you're lookin' at a strong set of hands." She had his full attention. Seeing as men sometimes didn't notice what was under their noses unless it smelled high, she decided to give him a good impression of the rest of herself. "Matter of fact, I'm strong all over. I just don't appear so. I ain't never had a back problem and my brain is quick on complications."

"Quick on being slick you mean."

"Nope, that's not what I mean a'tall," she said with undue calm while keeping an eye on him, liking what she was seeing. She was coming close to having wrong-way female thoughts about how good he looked, how much man there was packed into his pants. She lifted her face and found him smiling at her. Caught, she sniffed. "I ain't havin' evil thoughts about you, if that's what's makin' you grin like a cream-fed cat."

"Wouldn't do you any good if you were. You're not my type."

"That's a good thing for both of us, ain't it?" She let a fine friendly smile light up her expression to cover hurt feelings and held it until she thought her face would crack. She didn't have the time or wherewithal to study on him at the moment. It was just as well he didn't know how she was when she set her mind to something. "You got any objection to Maydean watching Willie-Boy and Dorie after breakfast while I check with one of them seafood houses? Like as not they'll put me to work and I can have your seventy dollars by nightfall."

Mentally calculating the proposed arrangement six different ways, Gage refilled his cup from the percolator. Hers was a simple request. No short end of the stick for either of them. "I've no objection. But Dorie can look after herself." His tone softened when he said his daughter's name.

"Dorie's self-sufficient, all right," Phoebe said, being agreeable. Lor! The child couldn't look after herself coming or going. Men were blind to the day-to-day responsibility of child rearing. "I'll tell Maydean not to boss Dorie while I'm gettin' up your money," she said, which had the effect of making him scour her with one of his probing once-overs.

Emboldened by the way he was looking at her, thinking that no doubt he was noticing how fresh and neat she was of a morning, Phoebe continued. "I reckon I'll be back in time to fix you a good supper. Anybody asks me, I'm sure gonna tell 'em how good and kind you been being to Willie-Boy, allowin' him to stay here and all."

He muttered an epithet beneath his breath and went out the back door, work boots thudding on the porch. On the path he stopped for a minute, shaking his head. He should've looked at it *seven* different ways, he thought. Phoebe Hawley had a tongue too clever for her head. She'd somehow talked herself into his everyday life. And he was beginning to like it, he concluded in resigned misery.

Watching him stop, seeing him shake his head, Phoebe divined Gage was awed by his good fortune and was trying to absorb it. It wasn't every day that a man wrecked a stranger's truck, then found himself enjoying that same stranger's talent as a cook.

She went to get the letter. On her way walking to the seafood house, she would put it in the mailbox by the gate. Ma would sure be happy to learn she'd found them a place.

THE SUN WAS JUST giving the sky a good pink color by the time Phoebe approached the first of the seafood houses. A group of women were filing through the opened door. Phoebe got in line behind them. A man stopped her just as she entered the building.

"Hey! Hold it. Who're you?"

"Phoebe Hawley. I'm lookin' to pick or shuck."

"Where'd you come from?"

"Gage Morgan sent me down here." The man's name was sewn on his shirt above his pocket. "Gage said for me to see Hank. You know Gage Morgan, don't you?" Her nose was twitching. The smell of the sea filled the concrete building. Years of it. Phoebe resisted the urge to pinch closed her nose.

"Everybody knows Gage."

"Well, then?"

"You ever pick before?"

"Sure have." No sense being dicey with words, she thought, or pointing out it was cotton.

"You're not from around here."

That was the trouble with small towns, thought Phoebe, everybody knew everybody. "Sure ain't. We came down from Cottontown. To help Gage with Dorie and the house and all. What with his wife dying . . ."

Hank shook his head. "That was a tragedy, Velma drowning. Gage took it hard."

"He ain't recovered yet," said Phoebe, looking properly sad.

"I pay ninety-five cents a pound white, sixty-five cents a pound for claw. That satisfy you?"

Why, picking crabs was just like picking cotton, thought Phoebe, feeling reassured. You got paid on what you picked. She nodded.

"Okay. Through there. Stout will show you where to sit."

Stout was just that; she had a big square torso below a short neck that held up a round face that displayed a permanent frown crease between her brows. Stout put Phoebe at a long metal table on which was piled hundreds and hundreds of boiled crabs, backs off. When Phoebe sat down she couldn't see over the mountain of seafood to the worker on the opposite side who shared the table with her. She picked up a crab and looked at it. It didn't resemble any picture she'd ever seen in *National Geographic*. In the first place it was dead. It wasn't the kind of creature a sensible person would eat.

She got up and went around the table. Her table mate had a pleasant face. Phoebe cleared her throat. The woman looked up. Phoebe said, "You got children?"

"Got seven."

"I got two. One's sick, I need money and I ain't never picked a crab before. I only picked cotton and shucked corn."

The woman laughed. "Better not let Stout hear that. You got a picker?" Phoebe said no. The woman reached into her apron pocket and handed Phoebe a set of nut pickers. "Use them like this." She demonstrated, breaking open a crab and plucking out the meat. "White meat goes in the clear plastic tubs, claw in the brown. Stout'll come around and collect your full tubs and give you a chit for every pound. You turn in your chits to Hank and he pays you at the end of the day."

"What time do we get off?"

"When all the crabs are picked."

"Lor! I got to be home before dinner."

"You will be. This here is a short run."

Phoebe couldn't imagine ever wanting to see a long run. "How many pounds does a good picker pick?" she asked.

"The best pickers? Forty, fifty pounds a shift. That's when the crabs are running. You'd better get started. Stout's looking this way."

Phoebe learned about crabs. Cooked, they were juicy, sticky, sharp-edged and often hot as they came to the picking tables direct from the huge steam pots out back. They had a sweet, fishy smell that got into her head and stayed there. No sooner was the pile down to where she could see her table mate, Essie, when Stout came and dumped another huge bucket atop the table. The crabs that fell to Phoebe seemed to get smaller, the meat more difficult to reach. At two o'clock the last crab had been picked. She turned in her chits and collected thirteen dollars and seventy-five cents. Hank counted out the money.

"Had an off day, did you?" he asked.

Phoebe listened for displeasure in his tone. There wasn't any. She smiled wearily.

"I been away from pickin' for a while. My fingers are rusty. Reckon I'll have a better day tomorrow." She folded the bills into her change purse. It was the first money she'd earned in months. She didn't want to have to hand it over to Gage Morgan. That'd just put her closer to getting out of his house. All the way back to the junkyard she examined first one plot then another.

The only certain thought she had was that she didn't want to look at, pick at or smell another crab.

The house was quiet. On the kitchen table were breakfast dishes. Phoebe fumed. She'd told Maydean to wash up. Willie-Boy wasn't in bed. Phoebe went along the path far enough to see that the doors to the welding shed were open. On the breeze she could hear the ping of metal on metal. That took care of the whereabouts of Gage Morgan.

She heard laughter and squeals. Maydean's cackle. Willie-Boy's yelp. Dorie's laughter was more musical. She found the youngsters lying flat out on the rickety wharf, their heads hanging over the edge. Willie-Boy was without his shirt. Maydean had cut off a pair of pants so short immodest parts of her were hanging out. "Maydean Hawley! Is this your idea of being mindful!"

"Phoebe!" Maydean scrambled to her feet. "Lookit. We're crabbin'. Dorie showed us how. You tie a chicken neck to a string—"

Crabbing! "You wasted a good boiling chicken neck on a crab? Maydean, I oughta tear into you. And Willie-Boy was supposed to stay in bed. Throw them crabs back in the bay," she ordered, trying not to notice the washer tub full of the things. "Willie-Boy, put your shirt on."

"I didn't move much, Phoebe. I just laid down here. I feel fine."

"I'm not throwing my crabs back." Dorie stood by the tub. "Daddy likes crab gumbo. It's his favorite food ever."

"Did he say that?"

"He said it every time my mother cooked it."

Phoebe wasn't of a mind to compete with a dead woman. Neither was she of a mind to incur the displeasure of Gage Morgan. She reckoned if he was hungry for crab gumbo . . . "Tote that tub up to the back porch then. Maydean, you got dishes to wash. But first you put on some decent clothes. You've ruined a fair good pair of slacks, cuttin' them off like that."

"I ain't. Everybody wears shorts like this. If you'd buy me a swim suit, I wouldn'ta had to cut 'em up."

"I'm going to buy you something, Maydean. First loose money I get, I'm goin' to buy you a shroud. Now get up to the house, like I said."

"Since I feel so good, can I stay here and keep crabbin' with Dorie?" asked Willie-Boy.

"Since you feel so good, I reckon you can take a swat on your behind for not mindin' me. Dorie too, for coaxin' you outta bed."

"I wish I was home with Ma."

"I wish you all were home with your ma," said Dorie, aiming at Phoebe. "You're not my boss. My daddy lets me do what I want."

"Your daddy ain't got rightful sense."

"I'm going to tell him you said that."

Phoebe glared at the girl. "I don't hold with tattlin'." She also didn't hold with smelling high, which she did. "I'm goin' to take a bath. When I'm done, that kitchen had better be spotless."

SOAPED FROM HEAD TO TOE, Phoebe lay back in the big old porcelain tub figuring just how much of her money to put in Gage Morgan's big, greedy paw. Like as not, he'd want the whole of it.

The way to get around that was to get up some romance. Men didn't think straight once they were romantically inclined. At least, her brother Joey hadn't. Soon's Vinnie had her claws into him, he mooned, moped, thirsted and went off regular meals. All of that and the only thing Vinnie had going for herself was a pair of endowments that she displayed by wearing tight shirts.

Phoebe got out of the tub, toweled off and stared at her reflection in the steam-misted mirror hanging on the bathroom door. She couldn't go much wrong by knowing what she had to work with—smart women used what was available.

Her brain was her best feature. But it was invisible to the naked eye. Gage Morgan didn't appear the type to be interested in a brain.

Wet, her hair clung in tight curls to her head. She fluffed it out. There were those who paid money at the beauty parlor to match it in color and style. She had it for free. That was one good point. Her neck was long and creamy, especially on the nape where the sun didn't get to it. All things considered, she had a nice neck. That was a second good point. Not counting her knees, her legs were shapely and strong. That made three good points.

Phoebe's gaze dropped to her torso. The only failing she had, if a body could call it such, was below her neck and above her thigh. If it wasn't already, it ought to be a sin for a man to judge a woman by what she had or lacked, from nipple to thighbone.

Best thing she could do was to convince Gage Morgan just how much of a sinner he was.

She took a big shuddering breath and began to pull on clean jeans, a faded shirt, tying the tail in a knot at her ribcage.

Best thing she could do was to attack Gage Morgan at his purse line. Seems like, she thought, pinching her cheeks to give them color, everything a woman wanted and needed about a man was below his belt. The thought made her feel less sure of herself.

In the kitchen Dorie and Maydean were playing at doing dishes. Willie-Boy, they said, was watching TV.

On the back porch the crabs were blowing bubbles and warring among themselves. On the path to the welding shed, Phoebe stopped and admired a pair of gulls, wings spread wide, skimming the canal.

The sea gull knew all about its life from the moment it was hatched. Instinct told it everything it needed to know. The bird managed life without ever having a thought. The closer Phoebe got to the welding shed, the harder she wished she wasn't having the thoughts she was having. She was thinking about sex. She had always been above such things. Up until she laid eyes on Gage Morgan she had thought that sex was the least of it. She foresaw now that she might have been misguided. She wished she couldn't count every one of her ribs.

Emerging into the welding shed, Phoebe looked almost pretty. The blouse knotted at her ribcage made a brave show; still bath-damp, her hair was frizzed into corkscrews, her unseemly thoughts kept her cheeks pink. Not wishing to be accused of sneaking, she hallo'd in her clear musical voice.

Gage pushed his welding goggles atop his head which had the effect of making his hair bristle wildly. He watched Phoebe approach. He had mixed emotions about the situation in which he found himself. He'd taken in and fed a stray cat or two, but taking in stray humans was altogether a different matter. He was having trouble acknowledging that he had actually done such a thing. But he liked having his clothes washed, his food cooked, his house cleaned, Dorie looked after and kept from pestering him. Velma had never done that, but a man couldn't speak ill of his dead wife. Any bad saying about Velma had to be slyly done by others, or he was put in the position of defending her.

Gage didn't like being put into any position that cost him money or loose words. He leaned against the giant propeller he was repairing and waited to see which it was going to be with Phoebe Hawley.

"I worked up a storm at the crab house," she said by way of greeting. Gage looked good, she thought. Work sweat beaded on his brow and wet his arms, highlighting the thick corded muscles. If he was making-do with a woman, she thought, he'd sure have to take care to be gentle.

"Seventy dollars worth?" Gage had an odd hollow sensation against the idea that she might say yes, load her bumper and be gone. He couldn't countenance the sensation. Phoebe's pointed face and wide dark eyes might have belonged to any one of a thousand ordinary women. Yet it was touched with simplicity, a certainty and a splash of charming freckles.

"You're a man what knows the value of a dollar, ain't you, Gage?"

"I am. Better than most."

"I figured that. A man owning all you do, keeping it up the way you do. Working hard. I said to myself, a man like Gage Morgan sure does know about a dollar."

Agreeing, but growing skeptical, Gage nodded. Phoebe thrust out her hand.

"So, here's a dollar on account. That leaves me owin' you sixty-nine. Pickin' crabs is some different from pickin' cotton, but I got the hang of it now. Tomorrow I expect to double what I paid you today."

Surprise made a whole rush of words leap to Gage's tongue. "A dollar is all you earned today!"

"Nope. Made a tad more, but I got to keep some back for Willie-Boy's medicine. Howsomever, if you want it—'' He was looking as if he did. "Now that I got a job, I've got to find us a place to live. That don't come for free. Most folks ain't like you, lettin' me charge room and board against housework and the like."

"I never said—''

"I know you ain't," Phoebe rushed on. "Most good-hearted folks find words difficult. My ma's like that. She'd give her house over to any stranger that pecked on the door and be so overcome with pity for the poor thing, she'd like as not speak two words from supper to bed. I noticed last night you're a lot like that," she added, making sure the corner she butted him into didn't have any sideways leaks.

His face was turning red. Embarrassed, Phoebe thought, slacking up on her misdirected charm. "I'll let you get back to weldin'. Seems like the kids caught enough crabs to cook up a mess of gumbo. After it's to boilin' I thought I'd clear out a patch behind the house for a kitchen garden. That is, if you ain't got no objection. Not that I'd be here to see it a-growin', but those potatoes I peeled yesterday had some good growing eyes. Seems a shame to let 'em go to waste when they're just itchin' to sprout."

Gage had so much objection he choked on it. She was taking over his house, his land, his daughter, his . . . He surveyed Phoebe from under half-lowered lids. One dollar. She thought she had the upper hand. Thought she was fooling him. He was smarter than she was. He had to be. He was a man. A learned man, especially when it came to women. Velma had ripped him up one side and down the other with her ways. He hadn't balked then, but he was balking now.

"I don't care if you stick peelings in the ground from here to Mobile. What I do care about is the seventy—"

"Sixty-nine," Phoebe put in since he'd pocketed the dollar.

"Sixty-nine bucks you owe for denting my truck."

"I guess I could give you another dollar. Then mayhap we could call it even. The way you weld and bang an' all, you could fix your truck yourself."

"I aim to. Seventy dollars' worth."

"You sure are stuck on that figure," Phoebe said with malevolent geniality. "What're you gonna do, line them raggedy fenders with fur?"

Gage flushed darkly. "I know the value of a dent. Get out of my shop. I've got a living to make. I want you out of my house. Taking in transients is for the Salvation Army."

Phoebe's lips went numb.

Her dream was crumbling. She was expending energy making her chest heave and flutter and Gage Morgan was oblivious to it. A romantic-minded man would notice, endowments or not.

"We ain't transients. You're holdin' us hostage by stealin' my bumper smack off my truck. You think I like being here? Cleanin' and scrubbin' and cookin' in the middle of a junkyard! You're lookin' at a body who was made for better things."

Gage snorted. "I'm looking at a body that'd have to put on two pounds to make it as a toothpick."

Phoebe's heart tripped. He *had* noticed her heaving chest—and took it wrong. "You're a vile-mouthed man, Gage Morgan. Hell-bound, certain." Oh, but she was in the company of a man who needed educating. "I can't wait until tomorrow," she said, giving him a full blast of scorn. "I hope I make enough money to pay you triple on that blamed bumper. But if you keep aggravatin' me, callin' me names, I'm liable to get on the road, bumper or no. And if Willie-Boy goes to dyin', it'll be on you." She drew a breath to go on speaking, paused and shut her mouth.

Gage passed a hand across his forehead, smearing the sweat and smut. "Willie-Boy could've died all over this junkyard today. I had to run him out of here twice. He looks about as sick as an overfed puppy."

Phoebe decided she was getting used to Gage Morgan's good looks. So much so she was starting to see his flaws, things about him that could irritate. It wouldn't take much for her to start thinking penny pinching was a bad thing. Then there were his eyebrows—they were all spiky. Not to mention that he was using up all *her* good points getting her angry at him.

"If he came in here it was to get outta the sun. You should've made him sit still instead of chasin' him out. Anyway, you can't see his sickness. You got to listen for it."

"What I'm listening for is you to say goodbye."

"Hand over my bumper and I'll holler it loud and clear."

"I was taken to the cleaners once by a woman. Made out a fool. It won't happen a second time. Seventy dollars for that bumper or it can sit over there and rust to nothing."

"You're a lucky man," said Phoebe, grasping the impact of what he'd said, "if all that keeps you from dunce and fool is seventy dollars. I'll get it up, never you mind about that. Even if I got to hang around here and put up with your un-Christian ways till doomsday." Which would suit her just fine and then some. She turned away from him and sashayed out. Not caring if he was watching, not caring if she had mastered the hip rolling yet.

5

PHOEBE FOUND A RECIPE for gumbo on a package of seasoned rice. The good thing about cooking—or having food to cook—was that it kept the ghost of hungrier days at bay.

The bad thing about cooking was the crabs. Live, they were more worrisome than dead because she had to dodge their snapping claws until the boiling water closed over them. But the bounty of them, coming from the backyard so to speak, set her to wondering if there was any money to be made crabbing.

Willie-Boy wandered into the kitchen. "Phoebe, my back hurts." His face was flushed, his eyelids swollen. Phoebe removed his shirt. His back was fire red, sunburned.

"If it's not one thing, it's ten!" she exclaimed, exasperated. "I oughta tear into Maydean and Dorie good, for lettin' you stay out in that sun too long."

"It's not their fault." His eyes watered. "I wanted to crab. I don't like having to make out like I'm sick."

"You have to do things in moderation, Willie-Boy. Moderation. Hours and hours in the sun ain't good for you." She went to fill the tub with cool water and put Willie-Boy to soaking in it. "That'll take the sting out. When you finish soaking I'll make an aspirin paste to rub on your back. You'll feel better by morning."

"Are we gonna live here forever, Phoebe? I like it here. I like Dorie, too. She's nice to me."

"She is? How so?"

"She don't boss me like you and Maydean do. She said she'd teach me how to swim."

"Swim! Willie-Boy when I ain't around I don't want you gettin' in the water. You even think about it and I'll turn your fanny the color of your back. Now you stay in that tub until I come for you."

Maydean and Dorie were watching television. Phoebe turned it off. "You two find a hoe. I've picked out a spot to hill up for potatoes."

"I'm no farmer," said Dorie.

"There's a mess of things you ain't," Phoebe retorted. "One of them you ain't, is mannerly."

"I don't have to mind you."

"Neither do I," said Maydean.

"You're borrowin' bravery where there ain't none, Maydean. I got the money to put you on a bus now. Vinnie would sure be glad to have you back changin' diapers, washin' dishes and sleepin' on a pallet on the floor. You want that kind of life, you just say the word. I marked off a patch of chickweed that I want turned under. So what's it going to be, hillin' potatoes or Vinnie?"

Maydean flounced out. Dorie said, "You aren't my mother."

Phoebe met Dorie's eyes. "I'm not trying to be. But somebody's got to take you in hand, teach you manners, teach you how to take care of yourself. You don't even know to comb your hair in the mornin' or wash your face without being told."

"I wish you would leave. I don't like you being in my mother's room. That was her special place."

Phoebe softened. "Your ma's special place now is in heaven. She don't need that room."

"It was her dreaming room. It was where she went to get away from Daddy."

Phoebe had to ask. "Did she tell you that?"

"I just knew it. Daddy fussed at her. At night I could hear him."

At night. There were things that went on between a man and a woman after dark that no child should know about. Phoebe had the idea that Dorie had heard conversations she hadn't understood. "When your ma drowned, was she by herself?"

Dorie shook her head. "She was with a friend. He got knocked in the head when the skiff upended. He drowned, too. I could've saved her. But she didn't let me go with her."

The friend was a he, Phoebe was thinking, summing up in her mind what Gage Morgan's after-dark arguments with his wife had been about. She couldn't countenance a woman not taking to Gage Morgan. But who knew what went on inside a marriage. "Listen Dorie, your ma's in heaven now. No doubt she's keepin' an eye on you. Don't you reckon she'd like to see you brushin' your hair of a mornin' and keepin' your face clean, like she taught you?" She kept her eyes on Dorie.

"You think my mother is watching me? All the time?"

"Well, mayhap not all the time. I imagine heaven is a pretty busy place what with saintly choirs, and angels flittin' here and yonder. But no doubt the first thing your ma does when she gets up of a mornin' in heaven is look down to see if your face is clean and your hair is brushed." She watched Dorie pondering the idea.

"Can my mother hear me if I talk to her?"

"I ain't sure about that. Let me think on it. Right now I got to get Willie-Boy outta the tub."

She also had a whole wealth of things to think on. She'd been taking Gage Morgan's animosity personal. His digs at her about being womanly—why that was on account of his own wife stepping out on him. That put a different slant on things.

Most likely Gage wanted to get romantic, but cuckolded as he'd been, he didn't trust a woman. His man-ego was bruised terrible. Throughout the remainder of the afternoon Phoebe figured and figured, looking for a solution around a disloyal wife who was dead and buried.

Considering how little attention she paid it, the gumbo turned out tasty. She made corn bread, bread pudding and iced tea to wash it all down. Willie-Boy was too miserable to sup at the table. She fed him from a tray and left him lying on his stomach, arms and legs stretched out, like an unpapered kite.

Dorie and Maydean were still at the dining table when Gage came in from the shed. He washed up and took his place. Silently Phoebe placed food before him. He was taking to her serving him as if it was the most ordinary of things. Routine. That was a good sign. He spoke once to Dorie about the crab catch. Phoebe caught Maydean faking manners and trying to get his attention with puckered lips.

"Dorie, if you and Maydean want to watch *Wheel of Fortune* on TV, you can take your pudding in the living room, that is, if your pa don't have no objection."

Mouth full of buttered corn bread, Gage shook his head.

"I'm fine where I am," said Maydean, sugarcoating the words.

Phoebe bent low and hissed in her ear. "You ain't fine. And you're gonna get worse soon's I get you alone."

Scowling hard, she shoved a bowl of pudding at May-dean. Once the girls left the kitchen Phoebe made herself a glass of tea and sat down opposite Gage. The solution to Gage Morgan was crystal clear. She knew just how to ease his mind about herself, but it had to be done in a roundabout way.

"I don't like anybody staring at me while I'm eating," he said.

A hot cloud grazed Phoebe's eyelids. "I ain't starin'. I'm admirin'," she said brazenly.

Gage gave her an icy glare. "You can't soften me up. I'm not the kind of man that'd take a pound of flesh for what's owed me. Even if it was offered by a woman who could spare it."

Phoebe's gall rose. She swallowed it back. "I ain't offerin' you anything. And I don't need your permission to admire a thing or not. Howsomever, you been misinformed by somebody. Your looks ain't nothin' special to draw the eye. I was admirin' the manners you have."

His cynicism was expressed in one dark spiky eyebrow, arched as if it'd been plucked to appear that way.

"Day after tomorrow is Sunday. We Hawleys are church-goin'. I was just wonderin' if you know of a good Baptist church hereabouts. One that's right strict and preaches damnation against fornication. I ain't for loose fornicators."

His cynical expression faded, replaced by—Phoebe couldn't put a name to what replaced it. She felt her heart compress uneasily. He wasn't taking to her solution right.

"Who the hell do you think you are? To come into my home and pass judgment."

Phoebe was thunderstruck. "Are you a fornicator?"

"Don't try to cover up what you meant," he sneered. "You gossiped at the crab house about Velma. My wife is dead and I won't hear bad talk about her. Not in this house. Now you get your things—your brother and sister—and get out."

Lost! Everything lost.

Phoebe tried to speak and couldn't. Blood drained from her face, the paleness having the effect of making her eyes seem to take up her whole face. Her legs were trembling so she feared they wouldn't hold straight to take her into the living room to call Maydean or to the bedroom for Willie-Boy.

"What's wrong?" Maydean asked.

"Start packin'," Phoebe said.

"You got us thrown out! I knew it would happen. You're so mean-mouthed."

Willie-Boy was whimpering. "I hurt so bad, Phoebe. I feel like I'm on fire."

"I got to wrap you in a blanket. I'll fix you in a nice pallet in the back of the truck."

"Don't touch me, Phoebe. I can't stand it."

She wrapped him and picked him up. He cried, great gulping pain-filled sobs.

"Hush now. Hush." Phoebe carried him back through the house, the kitchen, ignoring Gage who was standing at the sink. She pushed the screen open with her hip.

In the truck bed she made Willie-Boy as comfortable as she could. Maydean was sniffling. Phoebe felt she was close to tears herself. "You stay in the back with Willie-Boy. I got to get my change purse and the keys."

Gage accosted her as soon as she was inside the kitchen door. "What's wrong with the boy?"

"Nothing," she said stiffly as she passed on by, went into the bedroom, checking for left-behind belongings and retrieving her purse from beneath the mattress. Gage blocked her passage from the bedroom.

"You can't get far without a tag."

"What business is it of yours? Move outta my way. I take back what I said out admirin' your manners. You ain't nothin' but a arrogance-filled bully. I ain't of a mind to stay in a house with a man who misdirects everything that's said to his own cause."

"It'll be dark in two hours. Where're you going to sleep, put up for the night?"

A rest stop beside a highway, Phoebe thought, heartsick, or a side road somewhere that was dark and scary. "I'll make do. It's none of your worry." She tried to push past him. The length of her brushed him. An odd restlessness shot up her spine, making her scalp tingle. She looked up at Gage. His face was expressionless.

"I know it's none of my worry. I don't know why I *am* worrying. I didn't mean you had to leave tonight—"

"You did so."

"Well, now I'm saying wait until morning."

"No sense to that. We're packed up now. Packin' and unpackin' don't suit me. I like to get where I'm goin' and stay put. I thank you for your hospitality, what *little* there was of it. When I get the money up I owe you, I'll stop by." The soap and man smell of him filled her nostrils undermining her strength of purpose.

"You're cutting off your nose to spite your face. You don't have any place to run to and you know it."

"You can't have it both ways, wantin' me to stay and wantin' me to leave. I didn't make no comment to insult your dead wife. I was just lettin' you know I don't hold with un-Christian ways."

"I realize that. I flew off the handle," he said, hearing himself allude to an apology he had no conscious intention of making. She was somehow digging into the silent space of his soul. More than that . . . incredibly, he felt his body reacting to her. He discounted the sudden tightness in his groin. There wasn't a handful of flesh on her. And he was a man who liked his pound of flesh.

"'Scuse me," Phoebe said, escaping the room and his closeness. The ripple in her body put her at sixes and sevens. She was talking Christian and thinking devil. And Gage stayed on her heels all the way to the truck.

He peeled the blanket away from a whimpering Willie-Boy and winced. "You can't go off half-cocked with the boy burned like that." He turned and faced Phoebe. "You're earning your keep. You can stay until you can find a place of your own."

Phoebe chewed her lip. "I hate to eat crow worse'n I hate burnt toast."

"Must be that Hawley blood you're always boasting of. Anyway, you're too good a cook to burn toast." He signaled Willie-Boy. "Haul yourself over here, son. I'll carry you back to bed."

Like a deer alert to every nuance in the forest, every shift in wind, Phoebe was struck with the metamorphosis in Gage. It hadn't occurred to her that he actually could be good and kind without prodding. Or display a tenderness, which he did in the manner he lifted Willie-Boy. She'd judged him on calluses, purse strings, bone and sinew. Now she had a different aspect of him to explore. Different and confusing.

Maydean scrambled down from the truck bed. "What made him change his mind?"

"Goodness begets goodness," said Phoebe, giving the only answer that arose out of her confused thoughts. "Get back here, Maydean. Tote that suitcase."

"Meanness begets meanness," Maydean huffed.

"I'm going to save you from yourself, Maydean. After you go to sleep tonight I'm goin' to snip off your lashes. Save you from the sin of flutterin' them at every man and boy you meet."

PHOEBE SOOTHED WILLIE-BOY, fed him aspirin and tea, and unpacked—for the last time, she hoped, if she had any say in it. And it looked as if she might.

The kitchen needed straightening; she went to do it. Gage had pushed aside dishes and had ledgers spread out. "Can't do my book work in the living room with the TV blaring," he volunteered.

"I can run those girls outside till full dark if you want me to," Phoebe said, keeping her tone neutral.

He shook his head. "Not necessary."

The way he was looking at her, talking to her, made the rippling start up again. Phoebe rippled all over. She felt it in her legs, her stomach. It felt good. There was a subtle change in the climate between them. While she did the dishes, swept the floor and rinsed out the dishcloths she tried to fathom the nature of the change. Now and again, out of the corner of her eye she caught him tracking her. The rippling got more intense.

She was finished in the kitchen, but she didn't want to leave it. She made two glasses of iced tea, put one before Gage, and sat at the opposite end of the table. The sun sent a few stray fingers of gold through the window. In the dancing rays, Phoebe's hair seemed to take on a life of its own, not unattractive.

"You change," Gage observed.

The rippling had got up to her throat and made it dry. She took a sip of tea. "I seem the same all the time to me."

"When you're not leading with your chin and barking orders, you look nice."

Coy blushing wasn't in Phoebe's nature. When she got mad her face got red, but pure-out blushing, a warmth that spread from bosom to forehead was a new experience. She suffered it now. No one in the whole world had ever said she looked nice. She couldn't cope with it. "The first time I laid eyes on you, I thought to myself you had a good straight nose and...and...tidily cut hair."

Gage smiled. "I had just come from the barber shop. But looks don't count for everything."

Phoebe was electrified. "You think that, too?"

"I know from experience."

"Me, too. Brains is where it's at. Brains and a strong back. I got both."

"Brains, a strong back and maybe a bit of cunning, you mean."

His sarcasm was light, but there all the same. Things were going too well to bite on it. Phoebe took another sip of tea. All sorts of ideas were racing through her head. Ideas like how she might do her hair to keep it from being so flyaway, ideas like maybe stuffing her bra with toilet paper to get a better shape. She discounted the last as a waste of a necessary item, but held her head up high so her neck might be in his full view. He took out a pocket knife and began to sharpen a pencil.

His fingers were thick, strong and nimble. Phoebe imagined his hands on her, but she couldn't figure a placement that pleased her that wasn't unseemly. "I got to bunk down somewhere else tonight," she advanced.

He looked up. A glaze, heightened by an inner chaos, lay on his dark eyes. "I'm not taking you into my bed. That's not what I was leading up to, not why I said you could stay."

Indignant, Phoebe's flashing eyes ignited. "I never had such an evil thought!" Oh, but she had. And, once there, it had stuck. "Willie-Boy has got to sleep spread-eagled. There ain't room in that bed for him and me and Maydean. I was aimin' to ask if I could bunk in one of them other rooms or on the sofa."

"Suit yourself," he said dryly, sounding as if he didn't believe her protests.

"I aim to." Phoebe could feel herself getting all fired up. The good rippling sensation was shrinking.

Abruptly, Gage stood up. "I'm going out."

Phoebe wanted to ask where so bad she had to clench her jaws to keep the question from flying out. Going to drink? To get a woman? He was fair stirred up. She could sense it.

"I'll see to Dorie," she said with a dragging heart. She listened for his truck motor. When the sound faded she moved about the house with the quiet sobriety of a person attending a wake. She seldom allowed herself to feel down-spirited for long. If it got to be a habit, that's where a body stayed. Down. But she couldn't seem to pull herself up.

Halfheartedly she inspected the rooms along the side hall. In addition to the room she shared with Willie-Boy and Maydean, were Dorie's room, two large hall closets bracketing the bathroom, two more fine-sized bedrooms, packed ratlike with all sorts of furniture and . . . Gage's room. Phoebe put her hand on his doorknob.

It wouldn't hurt to have just a look. Most likely his bedding needed changing, clothes hung. Men were notorious about keeping up. She looked in.

The huge bed was the focus of the room. It was neatly made with several pillows leaning upright against the leather headboard. Probably special-made, Phoebe thought, to accommodate his huge frame. Why, she herself wouldn't take up hardly a speck of room in that big old bed. That is, if it came to sharing it. Not that she would, but *if*.

An air conditioner framed in a window hummed on low. Phoebe stood in front of it reveling in the cooling air. Lor! The man liked his luxury. She opened the closet. The faint smell of scent and man rushed at her. She ran her hand along hangers. Not a single garment belonged to a woman. He'd cleared out all evidence of Velma except gossip. Somehow, it didn't seem fitting. There wasn't even a photograph on the dresser or on the walls. She pulled out a dresser drawer. Socks and underwear. No bobby pins, no half-used lipstick tubes, no nail polish. She searched into the depths of the drawer and found a small flat box.

Phoebe opened it and backed up and sat on the edge of the bed. There were baby pictures of Dorie, a lock of hair clumsily tied with pink ribbon, two baby teeth wrapped in tissue. Gage's love of Dorie must've caused him to attend to these small items. But hate or an emotion as strong, had erased Velma Morgan with meticulous care.

Why, years and years after Grandma Hawley had died they were still finding her things lying about, a knitting needle in a chair cushion, her long hairpins and wire combs on the dresser, a lace collar in the bottom of the ironing basket. Each finding had caused a remembrance, a memory portrait. Phoebe looked around the room. It was sterile of woman. The man wanted no remembrance. To Phoebe's way of thinking, that wasn't healthy, not for Gage and not for Dorie. She spent another few minutes on the riddle of Gage Morgan, then roused herself to clear off a bed in one of the spare rooms.

Later, long after the house was quiet, Phoebe heard the back screened door slam, Gage thumping down the hall. She turned over and went to sleep.

6

PHOEBE WAS AWAKE and dressed before anyone else in the house stirred. She counted herself as reasonable as the next person, but this morning she felt hostile. She'd worked it out. Gage Morgan had allowed her to stay in his house with a grudging spirit. After which he'd taken himself off to drink or lollydab with a woman. Phoebe couldn't decide which was the worst offense to her nature: whiskey or loose women or the man who indulged in either.

The facts stuck out for themselves. She'd lain awake half the night worrying about him, wondering who he was with and suffering slight stabs of jealousy. No doubt a single stab was enough to turn her soul black with sin. Gage Morgan ought to be made to pay for darkening her soul. He sure should. Atop that, here she was out of the kindness of her heart making a drudge of herself for a man who didn't care whether she lived or died.

While brewing coffee, Phoebe rattled pots, slammed cupboards and banged the wooden back door open to allow in the fresh morning breeze. She crept down the hall and listened. No one had awakened. Especially the person on whom she wished to vent her spleen. He was no doubt lying in his big old bed, snoring away. Her hostility thickened.

Taking the mop out of the pantry she shoved it across the floor. At the corner of Gage's bedroom, she became more vigorous, shoving the mop so hard to and fro that the handle bumped and scraped his wall. For good measure she thumped his bedroom door two hard licks. She heard him snort and growl, heard his feet slap the floor.

Phoebe girded herself for battle.

His door opened. He stood there buttoning his pants, his chest bare, his hair awry, his beard stubble dark and his bloodshot eyes narrowed to slits.

"What in hell is going on?"

Oh, but he had leftover sin written all over him. Phoebe fixed him with a cold condemning eye. "I was just gettin' the damp mopping outta the way afore the kids got up." She sugar coated every angry word.

"At five-thirty in the damned morning?"

"I got to be at the crab house by eight. Just wanted to make sure I earn my keep here, afore I go. Like as not if I didn't, soon's I got back you'd be threatenin' to throw us out again. I can't worry about that while I'm out makin' the money I owe you." She didn't mean for it to, but her gaze seemed of its own accord to latch onto the spread of dark hair on his chest. Her eyes followed as it thinned and trailed down into his pants.

He muttered a low oath. "You're another one. Damn it to hell."

"Another one what?"

"Nag."

Phoebe turned pale. "You like callin' people names, don't you?"

"I got a good name for anybody who wakes me up as rudely as you just did."

"Well, I'm sorry. I didn't know you were still abed. How could I? Your door was closed. I can't see through doors."

"I'll tell you what I see. You woke me up on purpose. I can see that."

"Don't know how you can see anything with them whiskey-coated eyes," scoffed Phoebe, nit-picking as far as she dared.

"I can see all right. I can see your chin coming at me. Keep it coming," he jeered. "Pretty soon you'll stab me to death. Maybe then I'll get my sleep out."

"Won't," she returned petulantly. "I ain't of a mind to bleed whiskey all over a floor I just mopped."

"Listen here," Gage ground out, "if I want to have a drink, I'll have it. You keep your long nose out of my business."

It was wrong, of course, to enjoy quarreling. However, Phoebe did feel . . . satisfied. Yes, quite satisfied. She drew her chin back and sniffed. "Get back in bed if you want to. Stay there and be vile-tempered all day for all I care. I got breakfast to cook."

"This is the thanks I get for opening my home to a bunch of road ticks," he aimed at her departing back. "If I had any sense I'd let you take your bumper and be gone."

Phoebe felt her heart stop. On no account did she want him worrying on that notion and laying waste to the rest of her life. "I got my pride," she shot over her shoulder. "I ain't touchin' that bumper till I got you paid off. I told you, Hawleys don't take charity."

"Hawleys don't take charity," he mimicked dourly, stalking into the bathroom to wash his face and brush his teeth. The mirror over the sink returned his image. He made a fierce face. Hawley pride. Phoebe made it sound like something packaged in red, white and blue. The skinny stick! She was driving him batty. She almost made him feel like he ought to apologize for going out and having a few beers. It was the stupidest idea he'd had in weeks.

The second stupidest. The first was thinking it would do no harm to let Phoebe Hawley in the door. He should've known she'd make a general nuisance of herself.

To his way of thinking a woman ought to just go about her homemaking business and leave a man do what he had to do. The problem as he saw it was that this was his home and Phoebe Hawley was going about homemaking duties when she had no right to them. He'd clear her up on that point, pronto.

In the kitchen Phoebe poured coffee and while it cooled watched the dawn coming, rising bright and many-colored above the horizon. As if brushing a blank canvas, pink rays slanted across the yard painting the old coop, and crept onto the porch. Phoebe filled in the picture with Erlene feeding chickens, Ma hoeing the garden and Pa rocking to and fro on the porch.

Now she understood why Ma sometimes got riled at Pa over the silliest of things. A body had to have a go at what was unimportant, because she couldn't always speak of innermost feelings. Maybe a body never could talk secrets to a man. Phoebe didn't like the idea of that. When she got herself a man—and she meant to have the one that owned this house—she wanted only to serve up truth.

On the other hand, as testy as he got, if she were to mention she planned to spend the rest of her life with him, sleep in his bed, bear his children, he'd probably faint dead away. Men, and she included Gage among them, didn't like to be defeated with love. It was better to let him think he was coming up on the idea by himself. She'd just help out with a hint now and again.

She ran a forefinger down her nose. It wasn't long. It was a good nose. Whiskey sure distorted a man's vision.

As if she'd willed it, the man of her heart came into the kitchen. He was unshaven, dressed for the welding shed and cutting grim looks at her. With good cheer and a steady hand, she poured his coffee.

"Even if you *are* a grouch of a mornin', I like it here," she said, watching to see how her first hint went over.

"I don't want to hear it."

Phoebe went from rapture to rancor. "Drink affect your ears like it does your eyes?"

"My personal life is none of your affair. Don't try making it so. And don't get to liking it here too much. The backside of you is what I'd like to see."

"My backside?" Her light-colored brows shot up. "I thought you liked women that run to fat."

Gage sat there, staring at her, eyes glinty, face pinched. "I can't stand much more of this. Or you."

"I was makin' a joke." She turned slightly, giving him the view and opportunity to change his opinion about her nose.

"You're witty all right," he said, still watching her, noting her soft smile had transformed her clever face. It highlighted a fine-boned slenderness. "I'm laughing so hard my ribs hurt."

He blew on his coffee and took a tentative sip.

"Liquor sure turns you into a sour man of a mornin'. Makes you blind, too." Hints aside, that was one truth in the open between them. And because she wanted another, she had to ask, "Did you get yourself a woman last night?"

Gage choked. Phoebe pounded him on his back. Pounding and measured the width of it. Heat seemed to radiate through her skin. "You all right, now?" The backs of his ears were turning pink as newborn flesh.

"Oh, I'm just fine." Abruptly he moved away from her, heading out the back door.

"Say! Don't you want breakfast...? Guess you don't," she muttered as he disappeared behind the pile of old tires.

She stirred grits into boiling water and wondered about his ears going pink. Some men were shy about women, being all talk and no actual "do." Gage must be that way. With a man like that, she thought, a woman had a lot of leaway. An exhilaration charged through her.

"YOU LOOK NICE AND SPRITELY, she said to Dorie when the child took her place at the table.

"Maydean helped me get the tangles out. You sure my mother can see me all the way from heaven?"

"Like as not she can. Won't know for sure until I get there myself." Phoebe put a platter of eggs and buttered grits on the table.

"You aiming to go real soon?" Maydean commented snidely.

"You know the trouble with you, Maydean? You're all mouth. Shut up and use it to eat."

Willie-Boy was at the table, too, feeling better but popping out all over in blisters. "What am I gonna do all day while you're at work, Phoebe?"

"Watch TV and color. You be nice and Dorie might give you a page outta her colorin' book."

"I'll give him two pages if he doesn't try to follow me and Maydean around like he did yesterday."

"Follow you around where? Besides crabbin'."

"Around the junkyard. We tried to play teenagers and he kept butting in."

Phoebe slanted a look at Dorie. "How do you play teenagers?"

"I get to be sixteen and Maydean plays eighteen. When somebody comes to buy something from Daddy, we put our hands on our hips and look like this." Dorie fluttered her lashes and thrust out her lower lip.

Phoebe glanced hard at Maydean. "Is that right?"

Maydean shrugged. "It's just a game."

"Well, today, you just better play dead, 'cause that's what you're gonna be if I hear tell of this game again."

"It was fun," said Dorie. "We pretended we put on makeup and everything."

"Maydean can't play teenager today. She has to iron."

"I hate ironin'. It's too hot."

Phoebe gave her sister a warning glance. "You iron up our Sunday clothes. A dress for Dorie, too. In case she wants to go with us come Sunday. That's my final word."

"I don't know where I can find an iron and ironin' board."

"I'll show you," offered Dorie. "I like going to Sunday school. My daddy used to take me."

"Used to? He don't anymore?"

"After mother died, he said God did him in. He won't go anymore."

God did him in! For shame, Phoebe thought. It was Velma Morgan who did all the doing, but she couldn't say that to the dead woman's daughter. Another cross to bear.

On the other hand, it was nice to know that Gage had a Christian streak in him. Looking at him, she never would've guessed it. Looking at him... She recalled him standing on the threshold of his bedroom. She felt an enchanting quickening of her pulse. It made her feel good all over.

As the sun's morning warmth fingered the junkyard, Phoebe gave out last-minute instructions to Maydean before she left for the crab house, mostly dire warnings and threats. But she satisfied herself that Maydean would keep a close eye on Willie-Boy and Dorie. "If y'all need a snack afore I get home, finish off that gumbo."

Once she was outside, Phoebe walked backward a few steps, keeping the house, the ragtag fence and unkempt yard in view. Her heart swelled. Lor, but it was wonderful to have a place to call her own—almost.

"Watch out!"

A hand reached out to grab her arm before she tumbled backward over an old piece of iron bedstead. Then the hand released her as if it'd touched fire.

"I thought you went to the weldin' shed," Phoebe accused.

"I did. But I had to open the gate. Damn! Why am I explaining to you?"

"Maybe you like explainin'," she threw at him with a puritanical glare. "Maybe you ought to go finish your coffee. Maybe your mind is still muddled from liquor. Maybe you ought to clear out this front area afore a body comes along and breaks a leg and sues the pants off you." She rubbed her arm where he'd grasped her.

He stiffened. "That's how your mind works, eh? Always hinting about suing decent folks. Maybe you ought to watch where you're going. Maybe you ought to just go, period."

"Aim to," Phoebe said before she pushed him beyond redemption. She scurried out the gate to work, leaving him standing like an unbending board.

The hairs on her neck prickled. He was watching her no doubt. There was no sense attempting the hip swaying. The mood he was in would leave the attempt wasted. She was going to have to do something about his attitude. Gage Morgan was getting less friendly by the hour.

At the crab house, she slipped into her chair and nodded to Essie. Stout piled crabs in front of her and Phoebe began picking. The crabs got smaller and smaller, harder to pick. It took longer to get up a pound. When Stout brought another batch of crabs, even smaller, Phoebe complained.

"Hey. I want some of them big ones. I can't make no money tryin' to pull meat outta these bitty things."

"Last hired gets the littlest. Ain't fair to the other pickers to give you the best."

"How long does a body have to work here afore she gets the big ones?"

"Years," smirked Stout.

This is my last day of crab picking, Phoebe thought.

At one o'clock all the crabs had been picked. Phoebe collected ten dollars and eleven cents. While Hank was counting out the money she asked, "Who all do you buy crabs from?"

"Anybody who wants to sell 'em, as long as I get the entire catch. I don't hold with a crabber skimming off the number one shippers and trying to pawn off seconds on me."

"If I was to bring you a batch of crabs, you'd buy 'em?"

"You going into the crab business regular?"

"Plannin' on it."

"Well, ice 'em down and truck 'em to the back door. I don't pick up at the docks."

"I'll truck 'em," said Phoebe. She returned Essie's tools. "Thank you for the loanin'. If I stayed about I'm liable to use these on Stout."

Essie grinned. "Been many a day the rest of us had the same notion. Your boy got okay then?"

"He's better," Phoebe acknowledged.

"You planning on staying in Bayou La Batre?"

"For the rest of my life," Phoebe said with feeling, waving and turning away.

"Then I'm sure to see you around," Essie called. "Maybe at church."

Phoebe stopped. "You go to a good one?"

"We like it. And there's good programs for the kids winter and summer. Ain't a big church though, workin' folks if you know what I mean. We got a hand clappin', fiddlin' gospel choir, but ain't got a single member what wears a fur." She gave Phoebe directions to the church.

Phoebe strolled back to the junkyard stepping lively and high of spirit.

She'd made a new friend and had been invited to church. The gospel singing intrigued her. Maydean had a good voice. If she could get the twelve-year-old interested in music, mayhap it'd take her mind off boys.

She'd decided to go into business for herself and had a buyer for her crabs—that is, once she learned how to catch the things. Like as not by the time Ma and Pa and Erlene got here she'd be well established in business for herself.

The only thing out of whack was that Ma would certainly look askance at her Phoebe being under the same roof as a man without there being an understanding between them.

Phoebe shook her head. Achieving an understanding with a man who had *mis*understanding seeping from his pores at every word or gesture was as worrisome as trying to make a living. She knew what it would take: out and out seduction. Lor! What she knew for certain about seducing a man would fit on the head of a pin with room to spare. But she knew a woman had to use her body. Maybe even get naked.

Phoebe pictured herself naked, saw her ribs, her knees.

Better to think about the crab business, she decided. Still, all the way back to the junkyard, she practiced a hip-swaying walk.

THE IRONING BOARD was standing foursquare in the middle of the kitchen with Sunday clothes piled atop it unironed. There was no sign of Maydean, Dorie or Willie-Boy. Phoebe washed her face and hands at the sink then went to hunt them up. Maydean and Dorie were in the rusted-out shell of a car, Dorie behind the wheel, Maydean lurking at the mirror. Naturally, Phoebe thought. Her exasperation peaked.

"Where's Willie-Boy and why ain't you got the clothes sprinkled down?"

Maydean jerked. "How come you're home so early?"

"Because I can't trust you to do as you're told around a corner, that's why. Where's your brother?"

Maydean sniffed. "In the welding shed with Gage. He—"

"Oh, Lor!"

Phoebe entered the welding shed with a stone-quiet face of resignation certain she marched to disaster. She discovered nothing so cataclysmic as Gage grousing and running roughshod over Willie-Boy, for Willie-Boy was sitting on a stool and Gage was explaining the workings of a propeller. In her first start of surprise she didn't speak.

Willie-Boy caught sight of her and began talking rapidly. "I'm learning, Phoebe. Mr. Gage is teachin' me all about propellers. When I grow up I'll have a trade. Pa said I was to have a trade and—"

"That's nice," she replied warily. "But you're not supposed to be in here pestering Gage. He don't like to be bothered while he's working."

"I'm not pestering, I'm—"

"The boy's okay," Gage said, acknowledging Phoebe's presence, but only just. After slanting a glance at her, he turned back to polishing the machine.

All through her body Phoebe had a sense of good things, a feeling that life was pleasant and easy. Mayhap she wouldn't have to get naked to do her seducing. Gage's attitude seemed to have improved all by itself. Outside of threatening her with eviction, indulging in drink and being only somewhat God fearing, he seemed to have a good streak in him.

"I told Maydean to watch Willie-Boy. She should've."

"She was pickin' on me. Mr. Gage said I could set a spell with him. He said if I was to get out in the sun, you'd start up naggin' at him again, but I told him you wasn't mostly a nag, are you, Phoebe? It was only 'cause you're worried 'cause Ma told you to find us a place 'cause Aunt Vinnie is so mean to us. Ain't that right?"

Phoebe's heart began to pound mightily. Lor! If Gage got it in his mind that there were more Hawleys yet to come she *would* have to do naked seduction. She couldn't think of anything else that'd undo all the damage Willie-Boy had done in his five-year-old innocence. Gage's profile was clear in her view. One whole side of his face was a smirk. Well, she could undo that without seduction. She reached into her change purse and withdrew three one dollar bills.

"I told you I'd triple what I paid you yesterday. Here it is." She thrust the cash toward him, satisfied when the smirk diminished. He accepted the money. One thing about Gage Morgan, Phoebe thought, he didn't sneer at money. Still, there was enough snideness left in his expression that she felt obliged to add, "Hope you don't go wastin' that on drink. I worked hard to get it."

His jaw worked. "I spend my money the way I want. Though I suspect any man who hangs around you long enough is bound to end up a drunkard."

Phoebe's jaw began to inch up.

"I got to go to the bathroom," said Willie-Boy, slipping from the stool and hurrying out.

"I suspect you had a weakness for whiskey long before we met, Gage Morgan. Don't go blamin' it on me."

"I suspect you could make a living nagging the fur off a cat."

"Oh, I'm going to make a livin' all right. At crabbin'. Put that in your pipe and smoke it."

Gage smoked it. His mouth shaped a derisive grin. "Got fired at the crab house? Told Hank how to run his business, did you?"

Phoebe could see in his eyes, in his expression how he was making himself believe she'd had a comeuppance. She lifted her head with regal forbearance. "I resigned. I'm goin' into business for myself. Come Monday, I'll triple again what I paid you today."

Gage scoffed. "Going into business for yourself? Well, good. That'll improve my chances of collecting the debt you owe me. The way you're paying now, it'll be into the next century."

Phoebe's chin kept inching outward. "I got your number, mister. You think I don't have brains to see it, but I do. You've been savin' up your grousin' since your wife died. Savin' it up and just waitin' for somebody you could bully. You picked the wrong body. I can give as good as I get."

"No man in his right mind would pick your body. Hah!"

Phoebe stepped into his space. It was filled with the man-smell of shop oil, sweat and soap. She had to get Gage off the track of flesh and get him on the track to his purse strings. "You got that wrong. This body works. Every single part. A man in his right mind would appreciate that. He wouldn't be worried about what sticks out and has to be covered up. A right-thinking man appreciates plumbing that works, figurin' a healthy woman costs less. I got energy. I got enthusiasm. I got health. The man that gets me ain't never gonna have to pay for medicine and doctors. And I ain't got a cavity, not one. See."

What he saw were her dark velvety eyes with little lights behind them. Surprisingly dark eyes for one so fair. "Get out of my face." His voice held a slight huskiness.

Phoebe tossed her wealth of curls like a bright-crested bird preening feathers.

"Bloodshot and blind of eye. That's you, Gage Morgan. So you can just quit makin' vile references to my body parts. You're just tryin' to make yourself out better'n other folks. Well, you ain't. All you are is a man livin' smack in the middle of junk. You ain't even got the price of pride enough to keep up your yard. It ain't been mowed or swept since who knows when.

"A smart man, which you ain't, would sure keep his property tidy so as to increase its value.

"A smart man, which you ain't, would keep his eye on Phoebe Hawley, 'cause I'm goin' to be somebody. I'm goin' to be a woman in business for herself. With a fat purse." It sounded like boasting, but Phoebe didn't care. Nor did she care that her chin was so unflattering, so outthrust, it would serve as saucer to a cup.

Her breathless run-on speech had given Gage time to regain some composure. "You could have a fatted calf and you wouldn't appeal to me."

Phoebe clenched her teeth. He was still harping on body parts. He was paying her back for what he considered an insult, but she couldn't just let it pass. "You can't hurt my feelings. You know why? You're scared of me. I can tell."

Gage's jaw dropped.

"I used to think you had kissin' lips. Now I don't. Now I think you got flycatchers."

Gage closed his mouth, sputtering. "Get . . . get out of my shop. Stay away from me."

Phoebe gave another toss of her head. "I'm more than happy to oblige you."

She sashayed toward the door, arms swinging and hips swaying.

"You can twitch your fanny all you want," he called in loud hectoring sarcasm. "It won't change my mind about you."

Phoebe was at once fettered by excitement and stopped dead in her tracks. Practicing hip swaying had paid off! Warm with delight, she spun about, her face

alight with a high-voltage glow. "I ain't aimin' to change
your mind on any account. I'm *allowin'* for your opinion." She put one hand on her waist and cocked a hip
forward like she'd seen Vanna White do on *Wheel of
Fortune*. "Supper'll be late," she sang out loftily. "I got
to set out crab lines."

"Wrap one around your neck and use it for bait, why
don't you?"

Phoebe laughed. "Why, ain't *you* the witty one." She
lifted a hand. "See you at supper."

Phoebe's trailing laughter gave Gage a queer shiver
of dislocation. As she emerged into the slanting sun she
looked like a sprite, appearing soft and vulnerable as if
she needed him. He shook the sensation off. It was just
a trick of light. He got it into his head that she was up
to more than crabbing. A pleasant, albeit unwelcome
tremor passed through him. Not me, he thought.

No way!

The only things appealing about Phoebe Hawley
were her eyes. The rest of her was hardly more than a
scrap of flesh and a piece of bone. Get below her neck
and . . .

The sudden heat in his groin shocked him.

Willie-Boy popped from around a stack of weath-
ering lumber and joined Phoebe on the path. "You mad
at me?"

"I should be, but I ain't. I feel too good. But listen,
Willie-Boy, you don't carry tales about Vinnie or Ma or
Pa or Erlene to outsiders. Family stuff stays family."

"Ain't Gage family?" he asked, slipping his hand into
hers.

"No." Not yet.

"But you said we was cousins. You said the Bible—"

"I can feel myself gettin' mad at you Willie-Boy."

He jerked his hand loose and ran ahead. "You're gettin' just like Ma! Always undoin' what you say and mixin' me up. Next time Mr. Gage says you're a nag, I ain't takin' up for you."

"Willie-Boy, wait! Don't run like that."

"I don't care if I get sick. I don't care if I die!" He scooted off into some weeds where a boat was stored upside down on wooden supports.

"Then watch out for snakes."

He stopped running and began cautiously to make his way to the shade afforded by the upturned boat.

Phoebe smiled. Gage Morgan would make a fine upstanding role model for Willie-Boy. That was, once she got Gage's rougher edges smoothed out. Thinking that, she didn't mean in any way to be disloyal to Pa or Joey. But neither Pa nor her brother seemed to be able to hold down jobs. Boy and man needed work, needed to feel worthwhile. Having a trade did that for a man.

Having a trade could do it for a woman. Phoebe had it in her mind to be so worthwhile the joy of it would be unbearable.

7

"THIS IS WHAT WE'RE GONNA DO," said Phoebe when she had the kids lined up. "We're gonna go into the crabbin' business. Every day we make a good catch I'll give you fifty cents."

"How much will you get?"

"Don't fret that, Maydean."

Dorie was frowning. "You won't catch enough crabs to sell with just lines and chicken necks."

"I will. You wait and see."

"You have to use crab traps."

"You just show me how to bait these lines."

The child shook her head. "We have some traps. Daddy took them in trade. Then you don't have to stand over the lines. Besides, you can catch more if you leave the traps in the canal overnight. We can't crab with strings all night."

Phoebe straightened up. Working traps did sound more reasonable than trying to nab the crabs in a net. "You know how the traps work?"

"Everybody knows how crab traps work."

"You're so smart, you can show me."

There were thirteen traps, each a two-foot contraption of coated chicken wire built with a bait pocket that could be filled with fish heads or chicken necks. There were small openings through which the crabs could swim toward the bait, but the openings didn't allow for retreat.

Phoebe studied the traps and decided upon twelve. Thirteen was a bad-luck number. Having no fish heads or chum she baited the traps with chicken from the freezer. She couldn't bear to use the best parts so carved out the breasts to be fried later. She tied her skirt up around her waist and waded back and forth into the water, setting the traps several yards apart on the canal's sandy floor.

"Imagine. While I'm cleanin' and cookin', those old crabs'll be gettin' themselves caught. Just settin' there waitin' for me to haul 'em up and sell 'em."

"The best crabbing is out in the bay," Dorie said. "You have to use a boat for that."

"This suits me just fine." Phoebe went along the bank to mark each spot where she'd entered the canal. From the waist up she was sweating, waist down she was drenched. "I'm goin' in the house to change. You kids stay away from that water. You scare off one crab and you won't get nothin'." It felt so fine to be in business she decided to annex the threat and be generous. "Tomorrow's Saturday. I got enough put by that we can go into that Shambeau's Dry Goods. I'll buy you each a new pair of socks to wear to church."

"Socks!" Maydean flounced. "I want mascara."

"I want jawbreakers," said Willie-Boy.

"I've got socks," put in Dorie. "I'd rather have a coloring book."

"You're gettin' socks," Phoebe said. "I ain't squanderin' my money. Maydean, you get onto that ironin'. Willie-Boy, you water the potato hills. Dorie—"

"I don't have to do what you say. You're not my boss."

Phoebe sighed—for what, she didn't know. Dorie ran hot and cold, one minute she was nice as pie, the next as ornery as a mule. It was almost easier dealing with

Maydean who could always be depended upon to be her same old selfish self.

"It's my natural state to be bossy. You just take it wrong." Since bribes worked on children, especially Dorie, Phoebe bribed. "You want a slice of chocolate cake for dessert tonight, you get to tidyin' your room."

"We don't have any cake."

"That's what you know. I aim to bake one to celebrate going into business for myself. If your room was to get cleaned up, I was thinkin' you could have seconds."

Willie-Boy had been hanging back, listening. "Can I lick the icing bowl?"

"You and Dorie both, if you help clean her room." Phoebe picked up the pot of chicken breasts and left it at that. After a bath, she dressed in freshly ironed slacks and blouse and took special care with her hair, pinning it extra tight atop her head.

There was a good bit of traffic in and out of the junkyard all during the afternoon. Some folks stopped at the house. Phoebe directed them to the welding shed. A flatbed truck came and hauled off two of the great propellers Gage had fixed. When he came up to the house to do some book work she evinced not the slightest interest in him.

While he sat at his desk in the living room, she dusted and plumped sofa pillows.

"You want something?" he said stiffly.

"Nary a thing."

"Do you have to do that while I'm working in here?"

"Am I botherin' you?"

"You'd like to think you were, wouldn't you?"

Some folks got an inch and took a mile. Phoebe had already tucked her inch away for safekeeping. "This room's a fair mess. It needs to be taken apart and aired good. Maybe even painted."

"You're not bothering me. I don't let women get under my skin."

She gave him a wide-mouthed grin that set her teeth flashing, illuminating her whole face. Life was going her way for a change and her entire body seemed to vibrate with the smile. "You tryin' to pick another fight?"

"I'm just telling you."

"I'm just listenin'."

"You're up to something."

"Just earnin' my keep."

"You've been flaunting yourself at me, bones and all."

Oh! He was flinging trumpery of the lowest order. "I most certainly have not."

"I saw you out there in the canal with your skirt up around your neck, showing your underwear."

Insouciance replaced indignation. "Where were you peepin' from?"

"You don't have any modesty."

In spite of his attack, Phoebe's buoyancy refused deflation. "Didn't figure I needed any around you."

"That's right, you don't. I'm not interested."

"Course you ain't," she cooed, testing. "An upstandin' community man like you, in business for himself and all. It ain't likely you'd be taken with the likes of me." She fluffed another cushion.

Gage's brows knitted together. "You're a hard worker, I won't take that away from you."

Phoebe kept silent, waiting to see if he'd add more good things to what he'd just said. He didn't. "Which is the best windows to open in here to line up a breeze for the kitchen. I got some bakin' to do."

He went from his desk to open windows shaded by the great old tallow tree. In spite of his size, he wasn't awkward. He moved fluidly. Phoebe kept her eyes on him. The cool, shaded air swept in and caressed her. The breeze, his nearness made her more aware of her body than she had ever been in her life. Made her think about what she could do with it, uses to which she'd never put it—like sex. With Gage. She was amazed that she could hang on to thoughts like that and talk natural at the same time. "You want some iced tea?"

"Not now, I'm going to the bank."

"You reckon you could pick up some chocolate? I promised the kids I'd bake a chocolate cake."

For an instant he looked stern, forbidding. Phoebe thought he was grappling with the expense, with the idea of parting with cash.

"Anything else you need in the kitchen?"

"Eggs and milk. But I planned to—"

"I'll get them."

"Thank you."

He shot a look at her, seemed as if he wanted to say more. Instead he grabbed up an old briefcase, felt his pockets for his keys, nodded toward her and swung out the door. Phoebe followed onto the front porch, watched him to his truck. He wanted to know her better. She could sense it. He just didn't have the courage to ask her. Men were like that. She'd have to think up things to tell him.

SATURDAY ARRIVED WET AND WINDY. During the night, storm clouds had swept in from the Gulf, the wind so strong there were whitecaps on the canal. Phoebe worried about her crab traps.

Gage had gone to bed early the night before and had risen before Phoebe. When worry sent her to the kitchen in her night dress, coffee was perking and Gage was standing, staring out the screened door toward the bay, preoccupied.

Worry drove Phoebe to interrupt his reverie. "I got my traps in the canal. Will the wind tote 'em off?"

He kept his back to her. "There's not much of an undertow in the canal. Might turn them over, that's all."

"Dern!"

Gage canted a glance at her. He took in the shape of her beneath the thin cotton nightgown. Somehow the soft gathers made her appear more shapely, lissome. He forced his eyes back toward the bay which was barely visible in the gray sheets of rain.

"You're hoping too hard," he said.

Phoebe poured coffee. She took hers to the table and toyed with it. "Hope is extra. I count on work."

"Sometimes work doesn't get it. Sometimes work is just a filler."

"I know what you mean." She did, too. Mostly work was the only thing that could make time pass, keep a body's mind off more worrisome things. She wondered what Gage had to worry about. He had everything—a trade, land, house, food to eat, a child of his own, money in the bank. He didn't have a wife now, yet the one he'd had... Clarity struck. More than man-ego had been involved. His feelings had been hurt. Marriage meant stability, having a focus. It was hard to reconcile a man as big as Gage as having hidden feelings like that, of maybe having lost his focus. Phoebe gazed at his strong, wide back with new eyes. "Gage, do you get lonely?"

He was a long time answering. The rain beat on the roof, water ran in thick rivulets off the eaves. He sipped his coffee. "Now and then. Not so you'd notice."

He did miss being married! Even if it was to Velma, no matter what she'd done to him. Phoebe didn't know where to take the conversation, but some words, a comment seemed in order. She searched for one that would be truthful. "I do, too. Even when I'm in the midst of Ma and Pa and Erlene, Maydean and Willie-Boy. I feel left out. There's no accounting for feeling that way, I just do."

He moved away from the door and leaned back against the sink, one booted foot crossing the other. Phoebe sipped from her cup, suffering his probing inspection. She felt he was looking into her soul. Seeing what was there. She wanted him to see, to know. It was a moment of communion, silent, filled with tension and, to Phoebe, a thing magical.

Gage was seeing her profile, noting its fineness, the way wisps of hair trailed on her neck. Her lips were parted. He wondered how it was that he hadn't noticed how full they were. He was seeing the shape of her small rounded breasts, the nipples pressing against the thin fabric.

Out of the corner of her eye Phoebe caught the direction of his gaze. All he was doing was sizing up her body parts again! The spell was broken. She drew her arms off the table. "What're you starin' at?"

Gage jerked. "Nothing. You got anything to stare at?"

"Seems like I do. Your eyes are about to bug out."

"Hellfire."

"You like cussing at me, don't you?"

He put his cup in the sink. "I didn't aim it at you. I was merely expressing my opinion of where I'm at."

"Where you're goin', you mean."

"Right." He stalked to the pantry, retrieved a gray slicker from a hook and thrust his arms into it. "Hell is where I'm going. Crazy is where I'm at." He glowered at her, started to say something more.

Phoebe held her breath, awaiting the threat, the order to pack and leave. But Gage strode past the table, out the door into the rain.

Phoebe exhaled. The opportunity had been there to evict her and he hadn't. He liked her. That must be it. He wanted her to stay. He must've gotten a look into her soul after all...that was, before he got sidetracked. She wouldn't be so foolish as to hold the sidetracking against him.

She poured a refill of coffee and slipped outside onto the porch. The wooden floor was damp, cold to her bare feet. Wind-driven rain spattered on her face. She peered toward the canal, wondering what nature was doing to the traps, wondering if crabs scuttled about and got hungry in such disagreeable weather. For long minutes she stared into the rain, restless, possessed of the distant, preoccupied gaze of a woman whose thoughts were catapulting into the future.

"Can I have chocolate cake for breakfast?"

The images that reflected in Phoebe's mind dimmed. "Don't come out here Willie-Boy. It's too cool. Where's your shirt?"

"It has skin all over it. I'm peeling."

"I'll lather you up with calamine. That'll stop it."

"Then can I have some cake?"

"For lunch, not a minute before."

"Are we still going to Shambeau's?"

"With the rain and all, we'll have to see."

"Mr. Gage can take us."

He can indeed, Phoebe thought, *for life.* "He has to work."

"But you'll ask him?"

"I might. If you be a good boy and don't stir up trouble this mornin'."

"I'll be good."

Phoebe glanced once more toward the canal then shifted her gaze to the kitchen. Her cleaning and living in it had made the room homey. "Everything is gonna be good for us now, Willie-Boy. I can feel it. I'll bet every old crab is trapped and gnawin' at chicken right this minute."

"So I can have jawbreakers and socks."

Phoebe laughed and balled up a fist. "Here's your jawbreaker. Now go get dressed."

SOUNDS OF THUNDER rumbled through the walls of the gate shack. The building was little more than a free-standing closet from which Gage ran his business on Saturdays. From the door he could direct folks to what they wanted to look at, and collect for the purchase before they left the property. He sat on a stool in the half-light, leaving the single bulb unlit. The regular Saturday trade would be held back by the weather. He debated working in the welding shed, a thing he seldom did on Saturday. Truth was, he didn't feel much like working at all. He wished he'd stayed in the kitchen drinking coffee with Phoebe.

He had changed since she'd invaded his life. He was beginning to feel generous again. That alarmed him. He was enjoying having her around. That scared him.

He'd suffered the ordeal of Velma. He could admit it to himself. The only good thing coming out of that marriage had been Dorie. But he didn't know how to tend to Dorie's emotional needs. He feared she was too much like her mother. Since Phoebe's arrival Dorie had become neater, mannerly, less moody. As if Phoebe had put a spell on her.

He admired a woman who knew the value of money, how to earn it. Phoebe appeared to have an inside track on that knowledge as Velma had not. Velma had put his back to the wall, charging and spending money as if it were a never-ending flow like the tide. Velma had gone off and got herself drowned while in the company of another man.

Gage looked down at his big callused hands. He couldn't go on without a woman indefinitely, but Phoebe Hawley? She wouldn't take up the space between two button tucks in his mattress. Though it had been restrained, he had a healthy appetite for sex. It seemed to him that Phoebe had a fragility of flesh, that she was held together only by discipline and nerve. He couldn't see her having sex without wafting away.

Not that he was considering it.

He looked down at his hands trying to recall the last time he'd touched a woman.

He *was* considering it.

Best thing all around, he told himself, was to send Phoebe on her way. Force her against her pride to take the bumper. He'd be decent about it, he'd wait until she'd sold her crabs.

The rain stopped. Inside the shack there was no sound at all, except the noise of water dripping off the tin roof and the muttering in Gage's brain that said he was being a fool.

A truck came through the gate and stopped. The driver hung out the window. "Hey, you open for business?"

Gage tugged the string that turned on the light. "I'm open."

AT NOON Phoebe thrust her head in the door. "I brought your lunch. Fried chicken sandwich and a thermos of coffee."

Not once had Velma ever thought to bring him lunch while he was working away from the house. He didn't mean to be making comparisons, but there it was. "Thanks. I am a bit hungry. Haven't had time to take a break."

"You got to quit stalkin' outta the house mad of a mornin'. Eat a good breakfast. Business good today?"

"Fair."

Phoebe had scrounged a pair of galoshes from the laundry room. They came up to her knees. She had a towel pinned around her waist to serve as an apron and her hair was covered with a scarf. Controlling her curls was always a problem and in the damp air, an impossible task. The chicken sandwich had just been an excuse. Inside her was a force driving her to be near Gage. She'd fought it all morning. Now she was near him. More near than she'd hoped. The shack barely had room for his huge bulk. She cleared her throat twice, felt her stomach climbing into her chest cavity. "Gage . . ."

"What?"

"You reckon this weather'll hold the crabs back?"

He peeled the waxed paper from the sandwich. "Wouldn't hurt to leave the traps down a couple more days. You couldn't sell them this late in the day anyway."

"That's what I thought."

He ate the sandwich. Phoebe had the urge to be se-
ductive. She moved closer and brushed his arm with
her own, then she opened the thermos, pouring coffee
into the lid that served as a cup. She was so giddy her
hands shook.

"You're spilling that."

"Won't hurt this floor."

"Guess it won't." The red cup disappeared into his
thick hand. Phoebe liked his hands. He did heavy, dirty
work, yet the nails were clipped, clean. She had to put
her own hands behind her back to keep from reaching
out, to keep from placing her hand on his.

"I promised the kids I'd take them into Shambeau's.
We were gonna walk, but what with the rain by the time
we got there they'd look like mud daubers."

"I'll drive you."

"I was gonna ask to borrow my tag, just for—"

"I said I'd drive you." It was the least he could do
considering all the elbow grease she'd dispensed on his
behalf. Too, having made the decision to cast her out,
the small favor assuaged his conscience.

Phoebe pondered the tone of his voice. It was no-
nonsense and bossy. Like hers. "What will people say,
seein' you with me?"

He avoided her eyes. "Don't suppose they'll say anything."

"I mean, what will they think?"

"Why should they think anything? Seems to me I recall Willie-Boy saying we're cousins."

"He meant Bible cousins."

"Ah."

She was going to cut Willie-Boy's tongue out! "You
have mayonnaise all over your face," she said, and fled.
The heavy galoshes splattered mud a yard wide.

PHOEBE WASN'T LOOKING at Gage and he wasn't looking at her. But they were getting in each other's way while trying to herd the kids into the truck.

"I call the window," yelled Maydean, jumping in and hogging it.

"I'm sitting by Maydean," said Dorie.

Willie-Boy was all hope. "I'm riding in the back."

Phoebe grabbed his arm. "You're sittin' in my lap."

"People'll think I'm a sissy."

"They won't think anything if you don't sit on my lap. They won't even see you. You'll be a layin' on your bed until the rest of us get back. Move off that window, Maydean. Let me in."

"No."

"Maydean."

"I ain't been nowhere since we got here. I want to see."

"Come around this side and get in."

Phoebe scowled. What Gage was suggesting would put her practically in his lap. She was wearing her second-best skirt and blouse with black pumps. She gave the front of the truck a wide berth to avoid mud puddles.

"You want me to carry you?"

"A little dirt never hurt anybody." She climbed in without his help. He handed in Willie-Boy and got behind the wheel.

"Doors locked? Everybody ready?"

The kids chorused, "Ready!"

Phoebe couldn't speak. The whole length of her was aligned and pressing against Gage. He had showered and she got the full effects of that. Soap and after-shave wafted by her nose. It made her think about sex.

On the pretext of adjusting Willie-Boy upon her knees she stole a quick look at Gage. Her nearness didn't appear to be affecting him at all. She sniffed at his indifference.

"You say something?" he asked.

"We're packed like sardines. It's hot."

He rolled his window down.

"That's blowing my hair."

He raised it. "That better?"

"It's hot again."

"Should've let you walk." He lowered the window yet again.

Phoebe was a network of sensitive strings. When Gage pushed on the brake and gas pedals, his thigh rubbed hers. The strings that were her nerves zinged as if they were priming for a symphony. Once when he shifted gears his arm brushed the side of her breast. Her nipples peaked and began to hum. The sensation left her speechless. She couldn't even dribble a rebuke when Maydean craned her neck to stare and coo at boys on motorcycles. By the time they arrived at Shambeau's she felt as if she'd whacked a hornet's nest and got stung from eyeball to instep.

The children erupted from the truck. Phoebe didn't trust herself to move.

"You worried about your hair?" Gage asked.

"No."

"Are you going to get out here or go run errands with me?"

Phoebe jerked. Maydean, Willie-Boy and Dorie were disappearing into the storefront. "Lor!"

Gage took her hand and helped her down from the cab. "You need an hour?"

"Thirty minutes." Shaken, Phoebe reclaimed her hand. She forced her fingers to clasp her purse.

"Thirty minutes. I'll be waiting."

Phoebe took a step then turned back. She cleared her throat. "Gage, do you feel funny?"

"I feel fine."

It was all one-sided! She hated him. "I feel fine, too."

"You look fine."

She loved him.

"Your hair hardly got blowed a bit."

She hated him. First chance she got she was going to figure out how to bed him. That'd make him sit up and take notice. She spun away and sallied into Shambeau's.

8

ANGER FLARED ONE MINUTE, love the next as Phoebe banged around in the kitchen. She was fixing supper and handling pots and pans like percussion instruments. Love flowed in only one direction, toward Gage. Her anger flowed in two, at him and herself.

To avoid a scene with Maydean in Shambeau's she'd spent more than she'd planned. She'd bought the socks, a pair of nylons for herself, a knit shirt for Maydean because she refused to take it off, a pair of shorts for herself, a toy car for Willie-Boy and a coloring book for Dorie.

There had been the same crowded conditions in the truck on the way home. More so because of the purchases and a bag of groceries Gage had set on the floorboard. There had been a six-pack of beer in the bag. Phoebe frowned on that, but Gage was staying home to drink it. He had also bought ice cream and chewing gum. He was sitting in the living room drinking his beer while the kids sat on the floor clacking their jaws. It was enough to drive a body mad. She banged another pot to emphasize her displeasure.

The noise brought Gage to the kitchen. "What's all the clatter in here?"

Phoebe sniffed. "What clatter? I don't hear any clatter."

He cocked a brow. "You probably have the ships out in the channel thinking they're picking up distress signals."

"I wish one of 'em would come along and pick me up and take me I-don't-care-where."

"What're you mad about?"

"Nothin'. Do I sound mad to you? What makes you think I'm mad?"

He went to the refrigerator, retrieved another beer and popped the top.

That's two, Phoebe counted. "You sure like your booze, don't you?"

"I like a beer now and then, yes. I told you before, don't make too much out of it."

"I'm not. I don't even care."

"You want one?"

"I hate the stuff. Hope you won't be too drunk to come to the supper table."

"On two cans? Seems to me the beer is just an excuse. What's really bothering you?"

"Nothin'." Here she was heart throbbing, knees watery and he not only didn't notice, he wasn't reciprocating. "Everything is so fine and dandy I can hardly stand it."

"I'll just close the door to the kitchen, keep the noise down. Every time you slam a pot Willie-Boy jumps."

A surge of guilt scuttled Phoebe's anger. The doctor back home had said Willie-Boy's asthma attacks were sometimes brought on by emotion—overexcitement or fear. That was one reason she had him in tow. Vinnie had picked on him something terrible, kept him gasping for breath. "Leave the door open. I've about got supper done anyhow."

After the meal was served, Maydean and Dorie—cautious eyes upon Phoebe—washed dishes without protest. Willie-Boy's new toy broke. Gage got out a soldering iron and showed him how to fix it. Phoebe stopped clearing the table to give Willie-Boy a hug.

"What'd you do that for?"

"Because I'm proud. Look at you, learnin' how to weld."

"This is soldering," he explained. "Welding is when you wear a mask."

Later, after the children were bathed and in bed, Phoebe went into the living room where Gage sat, to watch television with him. He pretended not to notice her come into the room. But beyond his aloof expression, she could see the lines of tension around his eyes.

"That was a nice thing you did for Willie-Boy," she said. "Showing him how to fix the car."

Gage shrugged.

"Guess I'll go to bed." She emphasized "bed" to see if that would get a rise out of him.

"Good night," he said. He had a magazine in his lap. When a commercial came on television, he transferred his interest to the page.

That wasn't the response Phoebe wanted. It was unthinkable that all the thigh rubbing earlier had left him so unaffected. She tossed her head and fumed. He ignored the sighing and tossing. Phoebe got up and went out on the porch.

There was still a dampness in the air. More rain in the offing. She swallowed back a self-pitying sigh. She had a roof over her head, didn't she? Food to eat and money in her purse? This time last week she'd been scrounging for all three. But she didn't have that elusive fourth—a man of her own. Well, she had him. He was just being thick-minded about it. Reentering the living room she discovered Gage had been tracking her.

"Don't wake me up when you go past my room," she said.

"I wouldn't think of it," he returned in a tone overlaid with irony. Phoebe locked eyes with him. Her pulse quickened. She had meant noise . . . but he had meant stopping off in her room. She made a wild accusation.

"You've been thinking about it."

"Like hell."

His voice had risen a decibel. Defensive.

Phoebe pressed. "I ain't forgettin' how you looked at me this mornin'."

"Any time a woman parades half-naked in front of me, I'll look."

"Did I stir you up? Is that why you ran out of the kitchen?"

"I had to go to work."

She took the plunge. "You stir me up something fierce."

"Don't let it go to your head."

"That's just it. It ain't in my head. It's—"

"Shut up."

Phoebe's mind churned. A man didn't get so riled about a subject for which he cared little, she decided. So he must *really* like her, because he was so upset. His face was even getting red. He did like her, but he didn't seem to like the *idea* of liking her. Best she let him sleep on it, get used to it. She backpedaled. "Now I know why you're so sour of a morning. You go to sleep that way, it preys on your brain all night."

"What preys on my brain is how to get you out of my life."

Phoebe suffered an instant of sharp terror. "You going back on your word? You said we could stay—"

"You can. Just keep out of my way. And wear proper clothing. Just because you're skinny is no excuse to gad about the house half-dressed."

"I ain't the cause of your wicked thoughts," Phoebe said loftily, convinced now that she was, and thrilled about it. "Good night."

Head high, chin up, she sailed past him.

Gage glared at the set of her chin, the slope of her neck that was creamy against the dark blouse she wore. "Watch out you don't stab somebody," he gibed.

It took Phoebe five minutes to get her teeth brushed. She kept looking at her image in the mirror. Her face was flushed, her eyes wide and glowing. Why, she looked almost pretty. With utter feminine instinct she knew she could go naked into Gage's room. He wouldn't turn her away. All his blatant hemming and hawing was for naught.

She didn't see how she could go to him tonight. Somehow it didn't seem a fitting claim to propriety to crawl into a man's bed on Saturday night, and out of it on Sunday morning to go to church. Once she and Gage had an understanding it'd be all right. Lusting outside an understanding was hazarding the risk of sin.

WHEN IT CAME, the sound did not rouse her at once: the sound of sobbing. It seemed to rise, then muffle itself before Phoebe lifted her head from the pillow. *Willie-Boy,* she thought, *he's homesick again.* She padded into the hall. The sniffling came from Dorie. In the dark Phoebe felt her way into the room and switched on the ruffled bedside lamp.

"Dorie, you sick?"

The child pulled her head out from beneath her pillow. "No."

"Why're you crying?"

"You wouldn't understand."

"I would. I'm grown up. I know a lot."

"Daddy doesn't love me."

Phoebe rocked on her heels. "Of course he does."

"He likes Willie-Boy better. He's never showed me how to solder. He won't let me into his shop, either."

"Because it's dangerous. He doesn't want you to get hurt."

"He let Willie-Boy."

"Men think different about a boy."

Dorie turned her face into the pillow. "My mother loved me. She said so. Daddy never says he loves me. I want my mother back."

Phoebe sat on the bed and gently massaged the small shoulders. "You have to keep your ma in your heart, Dorie. You put her there and you'll always have her with you."

"It's not the same."

"I know. When Grandma Hawley died, I couldn't stand it. Sometimes I'd forget she was gone, and I'd think about somethin' to tell her. I'd go into her room and then it'd come on me that she wasn't there anymore. I cried and cried, just like you."

Dorie looked up, surprised. "I do that too. On my birthday, I wanted to show Mother my presents."

"I have a taste for hot chocolate," said Phoebe. "When I felt bad Grandma Hawley used to make me a cup and let me sit on her lap after everyone else was in bed. The only folks up were me and her and the night elves."

Dorie perked up. "What night elves? We don't have any night elves." She moved off the bed and trailed at Phoebe's side into the kitchen. Phoebe heated the milk and sugar, stirred in cocoa, then pulled the child onto her lap.

"Everybody has night elves. They sweep up behind the sandman. You know the sandman, he makes you go to sleep. That sandman is messy, his sand bags leak. All night long the elves have to run behind with their tiny brooms."

"No."

"Yes."

"What else do they do?"

"They get feisty. They used to play pranks on Grandma Hawley all the time. They'd hide her knittin' needles. Once they hid one in the sofa and my brother Joey found it. He sat on it."

Dorie laughed.

"Shhh," Phoebe cautioned. "Or you'll have the whole house stirrin'. I'll be half the night fixin' cocoa." She told another story and when Dorie's head began to droop Phoebe held still, allowing the child to drift into slumber.

A shadow fell across the table. She looked up into Gage's face, his expression a patchwork of curiosity and fear.

"What's wrong?"

Dorie stirred but didn't come awake. "She was missin' her mother."

Gage pulled out a chair and sat heavily. "What'd she say?"

"She's not used to her being gone."

"She looks a lot like Velma."

"You holdin' that against Dorie?"

Gage recoiled. "No."

"That's what you say on the outside. Dorie sees it different. You can't hold her up to the light of Velma. She's loyal to her mother, she doesn't understand about . . . about that other thing."

The blood drained from Gage's face. "Don't you ever—"

"You asked and I told. Fact is, some understandings work, some don't. Yours with Velma didn't. I ain't judgin' one way or another. Don't go holdin' it up to me that I am. I got enough on my plate with my own worries."

A muscle leaped in Gage's jaw. During the past year he'd been adapting to a world that had turned itself upside down. He sensed that he hadn't been adapting as well as he'd thought. He exhaled, his anger collapsing in dull melancholy.

Phoebe noted his look of distress. "Dorie needs somethin' to occupy her mind. Kids always get bored in summers. Why don't you get her some baby chicks? I could fix up that shed back yonder to hold 'em."

"And when she gets tired of them or goes back to school?"

"Why, by September they'd be big enough to scratch around on their own. You wouldn't have to do nothing but gather an egg when you wanted it." By then, Phoebe thought, Erlene would be in Bayou La Batre and have those chickens following her around like she was the Pied Piper.

"I'll think about it."

"Well, you're her pa, you know best." She slid her arms beneath the sleeping Dorie. "I'd better get her back to bed."

Gage insisted upon carrying Dorie himself. He moved around the table and lifted his daughter from Phoebe's arms. "I'm...I appreciate you comforting her. Truth is, I never could think of what to say to her after Velma died." In the taking up of Dorie, his fingers brushed Phoebe's breasts. His eyes suddenly shifted to hers.

Phoebe grinned, and whispered, "More there than you figured, ain't there?"

"Shameless hussy," he snapped. But there was more smile than bite in his voice.

The night wind began to creak the eaves, forecasting the onset of more inclement weather. To Phoebe it was the cheerful sound of her future.

SHE WAS TOO ANXIOUS to eat breakfast herself. While she served up toast and grits she checked off items on her mental list. She had a pork roast defrosting for Sunday dinner, a can of beer sitting out to get room temperature for beer biscuits, which was the only good use she saw of the brew, and was practicing what to say to Gage to get the use of her tag. As she moved around the table she kept bumping into Willie-Boy's elbow.

"Put your arm down. How can you eat like that?"

"I'm eatin'."

"You have a headache?"

"No. I like my hand on my head."

"This is no time for games. Put that towel on your lap lest you spill food on your good pants."

He put down his fork and one-handed, awkwardly spread the towel. Phoebe grabbed his wrist and pulled his hand away from his head. She glared at the wad of gum with dismay. "Willie-Boy, I told you to throw that gum out before you went to bed."

"I forgot."

"After you finish eating I'll cut it out."

"I ain't goin' to church with a hole in my hair. People'll make fun."

"You can go to church with a hole in your hair or stay home with a blistered fanny."

Maydean and Dorie snickered.

"Same for both of you," Phoebe warned. She eyed Maydean's chest over which was draped the new knit shirt. "You got underwear on under that?"

"My strap broke."

"Then wear one of mine."

"They're too small."

"Then find a safety pin. You ain't goin' into the Lord's house floppin' like a jelly fish."

It was Willie-Boy's turn to snicker. Dorie went to the fridge for more milk. Phoebe looked at her feet. "Dorie, your shoes don't match."

"I know. The night elves hid the mates."

Phoebe stalked into the hall, slamming the kitchen door behind her. The loud report made Gage stick his lathered face out of the bathroom.

"What in hell was that?"

"That was a bunch of heathens makin' me think un-Christian thoughts before I go to church!"

"Well, you made me take a chunk out of my jaw."

Seeing him without his shirt, smelling the shaving cream, altered and changed the direction of Phoebe's thoughts. "What're you shaving for?"

"Guess I'm going to church."

"With us?"

"You got any objection?"

Phoebe could think of only one. "We can't all fit in the cab of your truck, not in Sunday clothes."

"We'll take the car."

"Car? What car?"

"The one I keep in the boat shed."

Phoebe leaned against the wall. "Gage, are you rich?" She meant rich as in *really rich* outside of junk. It would put a different complexion on things.

He laughed. "Hell, no."

"How come you never mentioned you had a car?"

"It's one I bought for Velma. I run the motor now and then to keep the battery up. Dorie likes to ride in it."

All of a sudden Velma was becoming a household word. It was healthy, but it made Phoebe feel constrained.

There was no thigh rubbing on the way to church. Dorie sat primly between her father and Phoebe. Before the service Phoebe met Essie and sat with her. Dorie and Maydean sat with the Sunday school class. Gage kept Willie-Boy company in the back pew so there'd be nobody behind the boy to see the gap in his hair.

The preaching and singing of hymns restored Phoebe. She felt an affinity with her far-away family members. No matter what, Ma and Pa and Erlene would be in church right this minute, same as she. It was almost like visiting.

Gage knew a lot of people, and while he spoke with them, Phoebe went to wait in the car. She couldn't figure how he'd introduce her and she didn't want to spread the lie about being cousins on sacred ground. The sun was beginning to shine through the clouds. She put her mind off Gage and onto her crab traps.

Sunday dinner was a success; the roast just right, the rice fluffy, the biscuits light, the gravy smooth. There was laughter and no bickering. Everyone changed out of their Sunday best. Phoebe put on the shorts she'd bought. Gage came out from behind the Sunday paper to eye her up and down.

"Don't say nothin' smart. These are my working clothes. I'm going now to haul in my traps. I can't wait another minute."

"Better wait until morning," Gage suggested. "You can't let crabs stay in the hot sun. They'll die."

"I aim to clean out the back of my truck, keep 'em in the shade, like. Hank said he wants crabs early in the mornin's, by six, so he can have 'em boiled by eight when the pickers come in. At that hour I won't have to worry about driving without a tag."

"Don't listen to me then." He went back behind the paper.

Phoebe picked her way through the tall grass to the canal, stood in front of a marking stick and walked straight out into the water. It was cooler than she remembered. She found the first crab trap, tried to lift it and couldn't. The import of that struck her. Full! She raced back up to the house.

"Maydean, put on those sinful shorts of yours and come help me. There's so many crabs in my traps I can't lift 'em. Gage, did you hear that?"

"Me and everyone clear into the next county. You want my help?"

"For free?"

"I never work for free."

"Fifty cents then, that's what I promised the kids."

"Are those my traps you're using?"

She was at once wary. "I'm just *borrowin'* 'em."

"What about the bait?"

"I'm gonna replace it."

"I get half."

Phoebe was thunderstruck. "That ain't fair!"

"My equipment, your labor. Half. That's the way it's always worked."

"I figured you for stingy," she charged, attempting to recapture lost ground. "But I didn't figure you unfair."

Gage tilted his head, his lips curving, hinting at a smile just out of sight. "You've spent a week educating me on Hawley pride. If I allowed you the use of all my equipment and bait, why, that'd be like charity. Now that I know you better, I couldn't do that to you."

Phoebe choked on crow. "I've never been of a mind to admire a man who let a woman make his livin' for him."

"Me, either." Gage tossed aside the Sunday paper and hauled himself to his feet. "Think I'll see if that grass is dry enough to mow. I like the idea of improving my property."

Fried crow! "I ought to charge you for housekeeping," Phoebe said, searching haphazardly for a way to regain the upper hand.

Gage slapped a cap on his head and pulled the bill low. "How much?"

"Forty dollars a week at least."

"Okay, if you insist. But room and board'll cost you forty-five."

Phoebe recanted before something terrible and irrevocable happened, like the loss of all her as-yet-unearned cash. "I didn't say I would. I just said 'I ought to.'"

"Oh, I misunderstood. We'll keep on as usual then?"

Phoebe swayed on her feet. Victory had the unmistakable sour taste of gall. "I reckon."

TAKING THE TRAPS from the canal was heavy work. The sun bore down. The canal bank steamed. Maydean panted and complained every step of the way.

"Pull the truck up closer," she urged.

"It's as close as I dare. You want me to get stuck? Then where'd we be?"

"I want more than fifty cents. In Sunday school there was a girl who talked about a teenage beauty contest they have every year in Bayou La Batre. You have to get good grades and look pretty and have talent. I can sing and I can get good grades, but I can't look good on fifty cents a day."

"No amount of makeup can cover up a black eye, Maydean. You're fixin' to get two."

"When Ma gets here I'm gonna tell her how mean you've been."

"Ma ain't never gonna get here if we don't make enough money to send bus fare. Now shut up and lift."

Two hours later all the traps were emptied. The truck bed was covered and piled high with blue-green crabs clawing and scooting sideways, every one of them trying to bury itself beneath its neighbor. Phoebe raised the tailgate and leaned against the truck taking joyous note of her harvest. "I bet there's double any fifteen dollars that I'd get for pickin' the things," she said with weary satisfaction.

"Are we going to bait the traps and set them out again?" Dorie wanted to know.

"No. Whole chicken is too expensive. After I get paid for this mess of crabs, I'll buy up some regular bait." Phoebe moved the truck back into the shade and as an extra precaution, covered the crabs with an old tarp. "Dorie, you find me a waterin' hose. If they get to lookin' peaked, I'm gonna hose 'em down with cool water."

The crab harvest had been accompanied by the distant hum of the lawn mower. The sound had stopped, as if Gage had timed his work to end with hers. Willie-Boy came racing around the side of the house. When he saw Phoebe he slowed to a walk. "Guess what I did. Mr. Gage let me paint the fence!"

"Did he pay you?"

"No, but he hung a tire swing from the tree and it goes high."

A stream of water came their way amid whoops and laughter. Phoebe turned and was squirted in the face. Dorie threw down the hose. "Maydean told me to do it!" she yelled and both girls beat a hasty giggling retreat into the jumble of the junkyard.

"Wipe that grin off your face, Willie-Boy."

"I'm not grinning. Honest."

Gage came out of the kitchen on to the back porch. "An inspiring sight," he said.

Phoebe brushed her wet and dripping hair out of her eyes. The old T-shirt she wore clung to her body. She grasped it at nipple level and pulled it away from her bosom. Lips tight, she stalked past him into the house, wordless.

9

THE TASTE OF ACCOMPLISHMENT had about the same good flavor as a well-cooked meal, thought Phoebe.

She had gone to look at her crabs a half dozen times since the sun had set. They had stopped scrabbling and had settled down, folding their claws and blowing air bubbles. It amazed her that a creature so ugly fit so well into the scheme of things; amazed her even more that a creature so ugly would be the salvation of her purse and pride. God sure did work in mysterious ways when he was looking out for Phoebe Hawley!

Gage didn't appear to have any amazement working in him, yet she sensed that he, too, had that feeling of accomplishment. He had sat on the front porch watching the children playing "May I?" on the newly mown grass until she had dragged them in to bath and bed. He still sat there on the stoop, and of all things, smoked a pipe. The sweetish aroma of the tobacco drew her to his side. She sat on the same step as he, taking care to tuck her skirt about her knees.

"I didn't know you smoked."

"Now and then."

Phoebe glanced up at the sky. Stars twinkled. The moon was heavenly bright. "Hot tonight, ain't it?"

"Muggy."

"Yard looks good."

"I shouldn't've let it go so long."

"Why did you?"

He knocked the coals out of the pipe and ground them with his heel. "Lots of reasons." Velma for one, he thought. With her death, the manner of it, he'd lost his sense of well-being, the direction a man needed to see where he's been, where he's going. Seeing the place through Phoebe's eyes, those old feelings were stirring again. He was beginning to feel whole again, not as if his heart had been cut out.

"Name one."

Gage cringed inside. He could no more articulate his thoughts than the man in the moon. "You're nosy along with everything else."

"You're always callin' me names. Don't you like me one little bit?"

He laughed. "Can't make up my mind. I like your cooking. I can't get over how I just let you come in and take over."

"That's easy to figure. Your house needed a lot of soap and water. So did Dorie. No doubt that was in the back of your mind," Phoebe said, hopefully. "No doubt you took one look at me and decided I was good and strong and—"

"Nope, that's not what I thought."

"Oh. What did you think?"

"That you were the scrawniest, tattered-looking human being I'd seen since folks came out from under the last hurricane."

Scrawny? Tattered? Phoebe went rigid. "You must not think that now. You're always trying to feel me up."

"The hell I am!"

Phoebe registered the set of his jaw. "You like touchin' me. You just won't admit it."

He turned his head, facing her. "If I touched you, you'd know you'd been— Hell, you'd break in two."

Her want of Gage came from a primitive urge, took on an intense quality, an urgency. If she could talk him into . . . "I wouldn't. I'm limber. Size don't make no nevermind."

For a moment they stared at one another. In the moonlight Phoebe looked beautiful in a natural way. There was an allure to her face, the shape enigmatic, her dark eyes glowing. Gage jerked.

"Get away from me. Go to bed." He took a tobacco pouch from his pocket and began to refill the pipe. He fumbled with it and dropped it. "I said, go in the house."

Phoebe went, her mind moving faster than her feet. He wanted to do it. He wanted to and was scared to. She was scared herself. But it was in the natural order of things, of life, the reason why Woman was put on the earth. If that wasn't so, then why had God made Eve for Adam? Her problem, Phoebe thought, was that unlike Adam, Gage didn't have anybody telling him Phoebe Hawley was the right woman for him. Lor! She had to do everything herself. Planting ideas in a man's head and getting them to grow had about as much chance of success as getting a rose to sprout in the desert.

She put on her night dress and lay down on her bed. Waiting. *I'm going to do it*, she thought. Her heart was pounding so loudly she could hear no other sound.

It was long after midnight when Gage made his way down the hall and closed the door to his room. After midnight suited Phoebe. It was no longer the Sabbath. She had gotten through the Lord's day without committing the sin of fornication and if she had her way, come next Sunday, why, she and Gage would be well into their understanding. God favored understandings. So did Ma.

She crept out of bed and padded barefoot down the hall and pressed her ear to Gage's bedroom door. He coughed once. The import of what she was about to do rolled over her. Suddenly her face felt hot, her throat dry. She jerked away from the door and went to the bathroom. She wet her throat and splashed her face with cold water.

She looked in on Dorie, on Maydean and Willie-Boy. All were soundly asleep. *Dern!* she thought indignantly. When she needed a distraction they just lay there curled up like a pack of God's little angels.

She went back to Gage's door, put her hand on the knob. Gage would no doubt toss her out if she so much as took one step inside his room. She wasn't his kind of woman. She was freckled. Skinny. Scared.

What she was thinking about doing had the unreality of a dream. What if she got naked and Gage laughed?

What if he didn't love her back?

Her whole future hinged on that.

She took a deep breath and turned the knob, ready to flee at the slightest sound.

The air conditioner hummed and rattled. She slipped inside the room, closing the door so that the latch didn't click and made the trek from the threshold to the foot of his bed without notice. He lay with his back to her, facing the window. Phoebe tugged her gown over her head and dropped it on the floor.

Naked, she lay down on the bed.

Gage lifted his head. "What the—" he croaked.

"It's just me," Phoebe whispered.

Gage reached up and switched on the bedside lamp.

Phoebe's courage shriveled. She hadn't counted on light. Lying down the way she was caused her breasts to go flat against her ribs, leaving hardly a mound to entice him.

He was staring at her over his shoulder, his lips parted in shock.

"Turn that light off," she snapped.

The next instant they were in the dark again. Phoebe scrabbled for the sheet, got under it. Every nerve in her body throbbed to a savage beat. She pressed her length against Gage. He was as naked as she! She felt every muscle in his body go rigid.

The unexpected sensation of his flesh next to hers was like nothing she'd ever experienced. It made lights go off behind her eyes.

"Get out of my bed," Gage said, recovering his voice, but not his aplomb.

"I just got in it," Phoebe managed, still dealing with the awakening sensations, awed that the mere act of lying next to Gage could cause so much havoc to her insides. "I feel like firecrackers are goin' off inside me. Don't you?"

"This won't work." He couldn't allow it to work. The only thing love and loving did was let in pain.

"Cause you ain't tryin'." Her voice sounded odd to her own ears. She put her hand on his chest, felt the wiry hair beneath her fingers.

Gage grasped her hand. "Stop." The word stuck in his throat. He could feel every inch of her that was pressed to him. She felt smooth, silky. It took his breath away.

"Turn loose my hand. I want to see what you feel like."

"Don't . . ." It was a futile plea. He was burning internally with fires of long-suppressed passion. "I haven't had a woman in a long time. You—"

"That's good," Phoebe murmured. "I don't like a man that drops his drawers for—"

Prudence found a crack in his sensory perceptions, slipping through. "Out!" he raged in a whisper, sitting up, attempting to roll out of Phoebe's reach. She threw both arms around his neck, clinging with all her strength, her lithe body against his back. His brain registered the warmth of her flesh, the sensuous smoothness, the rapid beat of her heart. A guttural moan erupted from him. "Phoebe, stop. This is insane. We don't fit—"

Phoebe heard the conviction go out of his tone. She kissed the back of his neck.

"We don't—"

Her fingertips caressed his shoulders, feather-light strokes that trailed up the thick sinews of his neck and traced forward until she had explored his jaw, the shape of his lips. She bent her head and touched the nape of his neck with her tongue.

"Damn...oh damn..." he said, so softly Phoebe felt rather than heard the shape of his words on her fingers. As he lay back, she cautiously moved her leg over his, over his thigh, brushing him with the soft inner side of her upper leg.

"Lor!" she cried in astonishment. "Gage, is that your tallywhacker?" Before he could protest, she had her hand down there. Her fingers closed over him exploring, tracing its shape, its engorged length. "It's a miracle, the way body parts work," she said, full of wonder.

Her touch was sending delightful shocks racing down Gage's spine. He struggled for an inner balance, for air. His arms felt leaden, it seemed to take forever to move and clasp her hand to stop her.

"You can't . . ." he panted. His mind was numb, but far back in his brain logic said he had crossed an emotional brink; told him he was plunging into something far more entangling than a casual liaison. "Just a minute . . . Here, lie in my arms—"

"You sound like you're getting an attack of asthma."

"An attack of something. Keep still."

"I can't. I can feel the hairs on your legs ticklin' me. I wish I could explain how I feel inside. Everything is circlin', rockin'." Like a tempest, she thought, when she could think, for his hand was moving slowly at her waist, over her hip, back to her waist. Phoebe held her breath, expecting a comment about her bones, how little flesh covered them. He applied some slight pressure that drew her closer. His lips were at her brow. They felt warm, so soft on her, like new cotton. She didn't dare move, and yet, she felt as if she were floating.

His lips moved down her face, touching her eyelids, her nose, the edge of her mouth, her lips. He put his tongue in her mouth. Shock gave way to a wave of blissful pleasure. She strained against him, but still she could not get close enough. Her hands explored where he had forbidden. A moan escaped him, the sound as if he were being tormented, tortured. Then he was atop her.

She could feel him thrusting into the center of her being as if a floodgate had been opened. Thrusting, attempting a deep invasion. Strange heats burst inside her, little fires. Her body seemed to know just what to do. Her hips rose up to meet his, to accept him fully. She cried for him to press her harder.

Gage stopped in midthrust, a moment's bewilderment pulsing through him. Clarity dawned and he felt perspiration break on his arms and face.

"You haven't ever..." he began, tight-jawed.

"Please don't stop," Phoebe pleaded, arching her hips, flexing muscles that she had not known existed to keep him within her.

"You should've told me." He began to withdraw.

Phoebe threw her legs about him, locking him inside her. "I told you I was limber. Besides—"

"Phoebe..."

"It's the natural way between a man and a woman."

"I'll hurt you."

"You feel good!" she said with ferocity against a mounting panic that she had no feminine power with which to hold him to her.

Gage could feel his willpower unraveling itself. He lowered his head and pressed his lips to her cheek, her earlobe. "Tell me if it hurts and I'll stop."

"I will," she promised, sighing as he again began to rock with an erotic rhythm that reached to every sinew and inch of flesh she owned. Her virtue was now an alien and unwanted part of her body. When the sharp pain came, she bit her lip.

The eagerness of her body hung suspended for an instant, then a sudden release of abundant happiness welled up in her. She was out-and-out a woman now. It could never be undone. She closed her eyes and gave her entire being up to unmasking the heretofore mystery of sensual love.

GAGE WAS LYING with his elbow over his eyes. Phoebe's body was aligned to his. She was hugging herself, partly because the air seemed now to be unreasonably cool and partly because she didn't want to let any of the good feelings out. She was going over in her mind all that had happened. Discovering to her dismay she couldn't recall every minute detail.

"When do you reckon we'll do that again?" she asked, eager to fill in the gaps of recall.

Gage turned toward her, gently put his arm across her abdomen, wondering how he could have ever thought her skinny, when delicate was much the better description. "Too soon for you, I think."

"Well, what's proper?"

"Proper would have been not doing it at all."

Phoebe snuggled beneath his arm, glad of the warmth, of the way his body shielded her from the icy blast of the air conditioner. She was aware of a dampness between her legs, but ignored it in favor of lying next to Gage. She turned so that they lay face to face, hip to hip and ran her fingers through the hair on his chest. She discovered his nipples. She had an uncommon urge to take one in her mouth. She put the shameful thought aside, swirling over the tips with her fingers instead.

"Stop that."

"I was just seein' if they're bigger than mine."

"They aren't."

"They're gettin' hard!" Suddenly, taking one into her mouth didn't seem shameful at all. She pressed her face to his chest, flicked her tongue out.

"For crying out—"

"Ooooo, your tallywhacker's gettin' hard again, too."

"Phoebe, that's enough. I've got to think, figure out where all this is leading. I've got to get some sleep. You do, too. Don't you have to take your crabs to Hank's? Phoebe . . . stop . . ."

"I just want to catch up on the parts I missed."

"Missed? What're you talking . . . stop suck-ing . . . no . . . stop . . . Damn, you're making me crazy."

"Can I get on top?" She pushed him back and, drag-ging the sheet with her, mounted him, loving the deli-cious slick and smooth feel of him sliding into her; joyous that it now met no barrier. "Gage, is this proper or wanton, what I'm doin'?"

How could he tell? His blood had stopped circulat-ing. "Wanton . . ."

Phoebe had a sudden constricted feeling in her breast. She leaned forward, her elbows digging into his chest. "Are you certain?"

"No," he gasped. "It's proper. Your elbows are kill-ing me."

"Oh. Sorry." She sat back, balancing herself, exper-imenting with the newly discovered muscles at the core of her femininity. The activity elicited from Gage moans of pleasure. "What do I do now?" she asked af-ter she was satisfied that she truly did have control over so intimate an area.

"I'm not going to have the strength to get out of bed in the morning," Gage lamented, arching to press him-self deeper, to plunder the velvety sheath.

Phoebe sighed. "I have so much strength, I could clean this house from top to bottom and paint it be-sides." Exalted, she flexed her muscles. "Can you feel that?"

Gage placed his hands on her slender hips. "Phoebe," he ground out, "shut up."

PHOEBE WAS EVERMORE GRATEFUL that after Gage had gone to sleep she'd crept back to her own bed. She had overslept. The sun was well up and she could hear the faint sounds of the television, of Maydean and Dorie arguing. Lor! What if they'd found her in Gage's bed! She hurried to the bathroom and showered quickly.

Dispensing with toweling dry, she yanked on pants and shirt. She ached from scalp to toe. She wasn't certain if anybody looking at her could tell what she had done last night, but she had to face Hank and Stout at the crab house. She covered her body from head to toe, buttoning her shirt at neck and wrist.

Her face reflected in the mirror looked the same. The mirror was lying, Phoebe thought. She was different, she glowed inside.

She ran fingers through her tangled mass of hair, pinning it up as she hurried into the kitchen. Dorie and Maydean sat at the table, cosmetics of every description spread out before them, much of it layered on Maydean's face.

"Get that stuff off your face!"

"But I'm practicing how to put it on," Maydean protested. "I told you, I want to enter that beauty contest."

"You have to find a sponsor," Dorie said.

"Throw that mess away."

Dorie slapped her hands protectively over the treasure trove of lipsticks, eye shadows and tubes of mascaras. "No! This belonged to my mother. Daddy threw it out. I snuck it out of the garbage. You won't tell him, will you, Phoebe? He'll be mad. I keep it hidden under my bed."

"I won't tell him, but you can't keep it hid if its splattered all over Maydean. Where's your pa, anyway? I got to get over to the crab house."

"He went somewhere. Willie-Boy went with him."

"Who's watching TV?"

"Nobody."

"Wastin' electricity. Go turn it off. Then clean up this kitchen. There's milk and cereal spilt from corner to corner." She went out the door, headed to check on the crabs.

"Daddy said to remind you to wash bed linen this morning," Dorie called.

Wash bed linen? Phoebe's face flamed. The remains of her virtue were on those sheets. Lor! She raced back into the house. Gage had rolled the sheets down to the foot of the bed. Phoebe yanked them off. In the laundry room she started the washer and stuffed the linens into it, thankful she didn't have to stand there with a pounding stick or run them through a wringer.

"I'm goin' to sell my crabs now," she hollered as she made her way across the backyard.

"Don't forget my fifty cents," Maydean yelled.

Anxiety rippled through Phoebe as she backed the truck up to the rear door of the crab house where the crabs were shoveled into baskets and weighed. She must really be late. Usually there was a line of crabbers, waiting their turn. She banged on the door which brought Stout. The supervisor looked Phoebe up and down and frowned.

"What're you doing here, Hawley?"

"Came to sell my crabs to Hank," Phoebe replied. "I think I got about eight baskets worth."

"He ain't buying today."

"He is, he told me."

"He ain't. He sent the pickers home."

Phoebe felt dread begin to work its way up through her gut. She wanted to accuse Stout of lying, but no sound of laughter or radios came from the picking room, and she could see beyond Stout that the big steam vats were idle.

"Why? Did he say why?"

"He don't have to say why, he's the boss. You want to sell your crabs, you come back in the morning. Early."

"I got to sell 'em today. Who else buys crabs?"

Stout glanced over at Phoebe's catch. "None of the bigger houses are gonna mess with buying just that dab you're hauling. And anyway, you want to sell to Hank, you got to sell to him exclusively. He hears you sold elsewhere, he won't buy from you and you'll have to go clear across the bridge to sell." Stout glanced past Phoebe to the crabs. "You better get some ice on those, some of 'em are starting to go belly-up. Hank don't buy dead or dying."

"Don't worry, I aim to."

She'd get Gage to take her wherever ice was to be had. At the junkyard she parked the truck in the shade, sprayed cool water over the crabs and went to find him.

"He's not home yet," said Dorie.

Phoebe went to the welding shed to see if she could get her tag. She'd find the ice house by herself, she decided. The shed was padlocked on both ends. She discovered the windows nailed shut from the inside.

She returned to the truck, tossed aside more dead crabs. Those alive didn't try to pinch her even when she reached past them. She hung out the wash, waited for Gage, sorted dead and dying crabs, fixed lunch, and went back outside. She'd try to find the ice house, tag or no tag, she decided. She started the motor. It sputtered. The gas gauge read empty. She wasn't defeated yet. She'd siphon gas from the car.

Both ends of the boat shed were locked. It had no windows. The whole world was conspiring against her, Phoebe thought, dejected.

When the sheets were dry she made Gage's bed. Then she let down the tailgate of the truck and sat on it.

She was finished. Up and finished before she even got started. She tossed another dead crab onto the pile.

Fate wasn't abstract, she thought, it was something good, tangible, physical, her place in the world. Fate meant escape from poverty. It meant good-smelling soaps, regular meals, having her family at her side. She didn't see how she was going to deal with an absence of good fate. Only last night she had become a woman. She thought she had become invincible. It must've been a sin even if she hadn't done it on a Sunday. She was being punished.

A one-clawed crab scooted over the tailgate, landed belly up and didn't move. She wished she knew how to keep crabs from dying.

It was a balmy afternoon, not a cloud in the sky. A breeze flicked at Phoebe's hair, the sun bore down. She swatted at a swarm of humming gnats and gazed out at the junkyard which held Gage Morgan's treasures.

The huge pile of dead crabs had begun to smell.

Miserable, Phoebe sniffed and contemplated her future.

10

PHOEBE SAW GAGE approaching. Light-headed with loss and defeat, she didn't stir.

The odor stopped him several feet from the truck. He eyed the pile of crabs over which flies buzzed and flitted. Phoebe's cheeks were taut, the flesh made translucent by the sun. She appeared so dejected Gage was taken aback. Before him was not the Phoebe Hawley he'd come to know. That Phoebe wouldn't let herself be caught sitting in the middle of crab rot with her blouse buttoned up to her gullet and no feistiness in evidence. He paused long enough to take a deep breath. "What happened?"

"You can see what happened. In case you're wonderin', half of nothin' is nothin'."

Something twisted inside Gage. "Regardless of what you may think, I'm not the piper coming to collect too soon. Are those tears I see?"

"You see sweat!"

"Oh. Go in the house and wash up, why don't you? I'll bury that mess."

Phoebe didn't budge. "I can't pay any on the bumper, either."

Gage rocked on his heels, his eyes mocking. "Well, I'd offer to take it out in trade, but between Hawley pride and Hawley elbows, I might end up like Hawley crabs."

"This ain't no time for jokes! If you'd been here when I needed you, this wouldn't've happened."

"You needed me?" His eyebrows rose. "That's a departure from Hawley independence."

"I needed ice to save my crabs."

"Ah. Let me know when you need me for my own sake," Gage heard himself saying. "Things might take a turn for the better." And before she discerned that he'd laid his soul bare he rushed on. "I might consider fronting you the money for more bait, and a hundred pounds of ice should you need it. I know a bit about crabbing, if you're willing to learn."

"I'm not eating any more crow on account of you. Besides, there probably ain't a blamed crab left in that canal."

"If you're interested, I'll show you how to use the skiff, sink traps along the bay side of the marsh."

Phoebe's spirits lifted. "Get the bait and show me now."

"Can't. I'm expecting a flatbed with a propeller that needs repair. I've got to open the shop."

To that Phoebe applied the only bribe she owned. "Then you won't find me in your bed tonight."

How many times had Velma tossed out that challenge? Gage wondered. Scar tissue over old memories started to pain him. "Suits me. I haven't recovered from last night."

Phoebe was unwilling to accept that she did not yet have a fixed and solid perch in the universe. "You appear recovered to me."

"Do I?" He recalled Phoebe's ravenous sexuality, the way she had arched above him, the delicate veins in her breasts. He shook himself as if to shrug off a momentary enchantment. "Looks can be deceiving as I well know."

"If you're so wobbly, how can you dig a hole?" She leaped from the truck bed with offhand bravado. "I'll dig it. It's my mess."

"Suppose we do it together?"

Phoebe was conscious of a sudden need for him. She drew back from it as if drawing back from a chasm. "I don't want any help from you. Where's the shovel?"

Rebuffed, Gage kept his eyes fixed on Phoebe. Last night she had given him an extraordinary gift. Now she was acting as if they'd shared little more than a breakfast together. Because of Phoebe the discipline he'd exercised in staying celibate had evaporated. The power she had gained over him in so short a time activated his ego and gave rise to an acid tongue.

"Use your elbows, why don't you?" he sneered sweetly. "It'll go faster. If anybody wants me, I'll be in the shop."

EVERY TIME SHE DUMPED a wheelbarrow full of crabs into the trench she'd dug in the soft ground near the canal edge, Phoebe mourned. It was like burying gold that had gone bad.

When finally she went into the house, she met with a racket that could have caused deafness. Gage had followed one of her suggestions. He'd bought Dorie a dozen chicks. The chicks were cheep-cheeping all over the house. Doing other things, too. Yelling and laughing, Dorie and Willie-Boy chased behind the yellow fluffs, enthralled. Phoebe grabbed at Dorie when she scooted out from under the table.

"Get the mop and clean up behind those animals. This kitchen looks like a barnyard. Then put them in their box and out on the porch." Willie-Boy was rasping for air. Phoebe made him lie down.

Maydean was above chicks. She was parading around the house with a book on her head.

"Phoebe, has my posture improved?"

"Books are for the inside of your head, not the outside."

"You're just jealous. You'd never win a beauty contest. They wouldn't even let you enter!"

"They won't you, either, not with a pair of shiners."

It was an empty threat. The palms of Phoebe's hands were sore, with blisters rising. She couldn't even make a fist to wave in the air. Maydean was right, she thought. Her mind touched on all of the proud and beautiful things she would never be. Being clever had no beauty. Work might have a kind of beauty, but it took its toll on the worker. Love was supposed to be beautiful, but Gage had scorned it. Between his appeal and his menace, she was trapped. Love was on the side of the devil. She slid into a chair, folded her arms and laid her head upon them.

The book slid from Maydean's head. "Phoebe! What's wrong?"

"I'm tired. Tired of worry. Tired of work. Tired. Tired. Tired."

Maydean wrinkled her nose. "You stink, too."

A sob escaped Phoebe.

The cry so startled Maydean she blurted: "You go take a bath and lie down. I'll cook supper."

In her frame of mind, the suggestion held too much appeal for Phoebe to resist.

"HOW MUCH FLOUR do I use to make biscuits?"

Drowsily, Phoebe came half out of the pleasant dream she was having. "Two cups."

A minute later Maydean was back. "How much lard?"

Phoebe opened her eyes. The dreamy truckload of crabs disappeared entirely. "A cup."

"Then what?"

"Then I get up and cook lest we starve," said Phoebe.

"You feel like it?"

"Go put your book on your head and sit in front of the TV, Maydean."

"I was only trying to help," the girl said on a grieved note.

Gage put his head in the door. "Are you sick?" His expression was one of alarm, exposed for only an instant. Maydean scooted around him and disappeared.

"I can't find the time to be sick," Phoebe stated. She sat up and shoved her feet into her sandals.

"Did you get overheated? You should've worn a hat." She was wearing a thin shirt and the new blue shorts. She looked all legs. All limber legs. Gage sensed his own temperature rising. He wanted to say something to repair their argument, but he had never been one to speak loosely with exposed feelings and raw nerves showing.

"I didn't get overheated, I got mad. I came in here to get mad by myself."

"Maydean's making a mess in the kitchen," he said lamely.

Phoebe ran her fingers through her hair. "I figured I ought to leave it like I found it."

The idea of her going away was lost so far back in his mind, Gage was struck silent that she'd brought it up. There was a long time without sound, though neither of them noticed it.

"You're still mad at me," he said with a drop in vigor.

"I'm not mad. Ha ha. See, I'm happy." She almost was, what with all the attention she was getting from him. Her cynicism melted as she tracked the great strength of his arms, his torso.

"You've overdone it. Don't cook. I'll go after hamburgers and fries. Oh, here's a letter that came for you. I meant to give it to you earlier."

"A letter?" Anger, dismay, the stirrings of desire flew out of Phoebe. Her throat tightened. "From who?"

"Maybe those folks who're holding that job for you?" He glanced at the return address. "It's from a Hawley."

Ma! Phoebe could feel her body played upon by currents of hysteria and fear. Ma would never write unless something terrible had happened. A hundred expressions struggled beneath the surface of her features, but were erased before Gage could decipher their meaning.

"It was one of my cousins that had the job for me."

"Biblical?" he scorned lightly.

There was a sudden stubborn reserve in Phoebe's eyes. She closed the distance between them, snatched the letter from him. "If you're going after burgers, go!"

"You're back to normal."

"I'm always normal." She pushed him out the door and slammed it.

Once alone, a leaden feeling settled over her. She had the fatalistic feeling of being drawn from one wrong turning to another.

With trembling hands she opened the letter. No one had died. No one was hurt, but Erlene had taken Vinnie's baby for a walk, sat him down along the way and returned home without him. Then forgot where she'd walked. A neighbor had brought the baby home. To preserve his marriage, her brother Joey was loaning Ma the bus fare out of his paycheck on Friday. Ma and Pa and Erlene were to arrive in Bayou La Batre on Saturday.

Phoebe roamed about the room swallowing back panic. Life was playing a practical joke on her. She reread the last line. Saturday. Lor!

The letter revived her feel for possibilities. For survival. Her brain began to whirl with ideas.

Uppermost was an understanding with Gage. She had to manage it. In and out of bed, she'd be nice. She wouldn't allow an unkind word to pass her lips.

THEY PICNICKED ON THE PORCH, feeding scraps of fries and bread to the chicks. The sun was getting lower and lower on the horizon, painting the canal golden. Phoebe eyed the crab traps stacked at its edge.

"I reckon I was too upset this afternoon to take you up on your offer of teachin' me to crab right," she said to Gage in her sweetest tone. "I was just disappointed that I couldn't pay you."

"That was a fine catch to lose."

"You'll help me set traps tomorrow?"

"I'm a man of my word."

Phoebe beamed at him. "A lot of men ain't. They tell a woman one thing and do another. And I appreciate you being so good to Willie-Boy, takin' him with you today and all."

Gage listened and pursed his lips. He had no idea what Phoebe's game was, but her invention of good humor shone through her guile. Whatever her vision, he suspected she was absolutely committed to it. The knowledge strengthened his resistance.

"Willie-Boy's no trouble."

"Maydean is. You sure tolerate her well. I suppose it's 'cause you're doing such a good job with Dorie."

"That's not what you said earlier." He took out his pipe and began to fill it.

"I know you better now. I see how hard you work to provide for her. Kids ain't easy to raise. You being widowed, why, I reckon you're doing the best you can. You want a beer? I'll get it for you."

"I don't want a beer. I need to keep my head clear."

"Why?"

"Because I have the feeling I'm tangling with a wildcat and I'm bound to get clawed."

"What wildcat?"

"You."

"I ain't mean!"

"What have you got in store for me?"

Phoebe canted an innocent look at him. "Why, nothin'. Lor! What a thing to say."

"Speaking of saying, what news did that letter bring?"

Phoebe's mouth went dry. "The job ain't come open yet. Maybe next week. You mind us hangin' around till then?"

"I don't know if I mind or not."

Phoebe felt her heart collapsing in upon itself. "You don't?"

"I don't."

"Is it because Maydean stays in front of the bathroom mirror? I'll tan her hide—"

"It has nothing to do with Maydean."

"Willie-Boy aggravated you."

Gage shook his head.

Phoebe distilled their conversation and came away enlightened. It was herself! She couldn't bear it now that

they were so intimately connected. Fear had its own seduction and she couldn't help saying, "You still think
I'm too skinny."

"You're not too skinny."

Gage put a match to the tobacco and inhaled. He was
beyond mere flesh and bones. Velma's infidelity had
hurt him deeply. Her death had shattered him. For in
dying she'd never given him the chance to repair their
marriage. It was like leaving something undone. He
wasn't certain of his ability to cope with another rela-
tionship. He'd been trusting, easygoing. His attitude
toward love itself now had a faintly jaundiced edge. It
was Phoebe's hard luck that she was the first woman in
his life since Velma had died and so was bearing the
brunt of old injuries. He recounted these things, but he
didn't know how to say them.

He looked at Phoebe through a spiral of smoke. She
had remarkable cheeks and eyes. It was a face that
would last into old age. He caught what he was thinking and shunted away from it.

"Then why don't you know? I know. I like it here.
And I got you to take pride in your place. I'm good for
you. And, Dorie, why she likes me now."

"You're a fast worker, I'll hand you that."

Phoebe was nonplussed with the recognition that
Gage held himself apart from her. Suddenly, as if she
had willed it, there were dark circles of exhaustion under her eyes; the dark accentuating her eyes, which
gleamed as though what was left of her vitality had
centered itself in their depths.

The sole dignity left to her was to act as if she didn't
care.

"I'd better go help the kids get those chicks in the shack. Like as not we'll have to rig up a something to keep out chicken hawks."

"Maybe next weekend," Gage agreed.

Next weekend. Phoebe shuddered. Our Father, save us, she prayed.

She helped bed down the feathered chicks and two hours later, her own brood. She was nothing if not a positive thinker, and she meant to spend the night with Gage. But lying in her own bed, waiting for the house to settle she fell soundly asleep. She awoke at dawn, and then it was too late, for Gage was already up. She could smell the coffee percolating.

She dressed quickly and fingers flying, braided her hair which was as close as she ever came to taming it. Gage wasn't in the kitchen or anywhere else about the house. She discovered him down by the canal. He'd moved the skiff from its storage blocks into the water and was installing a small motor.

"I'll help you," she said, coming up behind him.

Gage started. "Don't sneak up on me like that."

"I didn't sneak." He hadn't yet shaved. His face was drawn. Phoebe worried that she was becoming too much of a burden. "You don't have to show me how to run that boat. I can figure it out for myself."

"I said I'd show you and I will."

"You look like it pains you. Anyway, you're not responsible for me. I can learn the crab business by myself."

Gage finished with the motor and stepped ashore. "You ever run a boat before?"

"I'm a quick study."

He took her arm. "Let's go back to the house. It'll be an hour before the bait shop opens."

Phoebe allowed him to propel her along. It was wonderful to have him touching her, even if it was just her arm.

They sat together on the back porch steps, sipping coffee, watching the sun rise.

"If I was back home and the mills hadn't closed, I'd be at work now," Phoebe said.

"Why is it you have the care of Maydean and Willie-Boy? Are your parents ill? Or did you have a falling out and run off with your brother and sister?"

"Not exactly," said Phoebe, treading delicate ground.

Gage cast a glance at her. "Not exactly? Either they're ill or they're not. Either you had a falling out or you didn't."

"Well, for sure, the falling out was with Vinnie, my sister-in-law."

"And what about your parents? For sure?"

Phoebe cleared her throat. "They live with my brother Joey and Vinnie. Erlene does too.

"Erlene?"

"My other sister. She suffered a fever," added Phoebe which was as close as she dared to hinting that Erlene was loose-minded.

"So there's a whole clan of you Hawleys loose on the world. By any chance did the rest of your family lose their jobs when the mills closed down?"

"We're good folks, hard workers every one. Ma and Pa have the care of Erlene and I've the care of Willie-Boy and Maydean. That's just the way it worked out. Even Stephen, three and three."

"I'm getting the picture now."

"What picture?"

"You're scouting."

"I don't know what you mean."

"I think you do. Willie-Boy said you were supposed to find a place. He meant for your whole family."

"There ain't nothin' wrong with that!"

"What's wrong with it is you took one look at me and thought I was a pushover. I let you in. I know how your mind works. You think you can sweeten me up and I'll let the Hawley clan move in on me. That's what getting in my bed was all about."

"I never thought that! Not for one minute! My aim is to make enough money to set Ma and Pa up in their own place."

"You're a good daughter." His voice dripped sarcasm.

"I came to you because I wanted you. You're the first man I ever saw I wanted. Ma and Pa didn't have anything to do with it. It was me. By myself. Why if Ma knew what I'd done, she'd be scandalized."

"And your pa would show up aiming a shotgun."

"Pa doesn't know the first thing about guns. And anyway, he couldn't make me take up with a man I don't want."

"Pity the poor man."

In the growing light Gage's profile was angular, strong. Moving outside her dismay, Phoebe noted how finely made were his ears. She reached up and stroked the outer curl. "Let's not fuss. I meant to come to you last night—"

He grabbed her wrist and put her hand back onto her knee. "I'm going after that bait. Now that I've got you figured, your success means as much to me as it does to you. I've got enough expense keeping up the yard and Dorie."

"You don't want to talk about what we did."

"That's right. And I don't want you creeping into my room in the middle of the night again, either."

Phoebe was scared she knew what he meant. It threw a flush into her brain. "I ain't up to doin' it in the daylight yet," she said, goaded by the need to keep the conversation, the intimacy, intact. But he was draining his cup, anxious to leave. "Gage. Don't go yet. I like sittin' here with you. I get the most funny feelin' in my stomach just lookin' at you and rememberin'. This mornin' when I woke up and thought of you, I felt like I was hatchin' a passel of moths."

"Phoebe, stop it. I like you. I like what you're trying to do to better yourself. You've got more grit than any ten women I know. It's your gall that's getting to me."

"I'm payin' my way. Gall don't have nothin' to do with it."

"Look me in the eye and tell me you weren't planning a coup."

Phoebe didn't know what a coup was. She looked him in the eye. "I ain't."

"So I'm not going to come in the house one night and find three more Hawleys invited to dinner?"

Blood drained from Phoebe's face. "It's your house. You'd have to do the invitin'. Gage—don't you like me one little bit? Personal?"

He emitted a self-deprecating laugh. "Phoebe, women don't often stay with the first man they've known sexually. Not these days. Once the excitement wears off the illusion of love is hard to maintain. No one knows that better than myself."

Phoebe heard the word love and leaned into his space. "I hope you ain't comparing me to Velma. Love is no illusion. Love is real. I can *taste* it."

"Oh, hell!" Gage said doggedly. "Look, I'll be back inside an hour."

Phoebe raced through the house to watch him out the gate. The truck paused and she thought for an instant Gage was going to back up, return to her. The truck pulled away. She let the curtain drop.

She had given him a unique part of herself. In return he had shown her a secret wonder of life, proved its existence. But now...

"I make the biggest mistakes," she cried forlornly into the air.

11

PHOEBE MADE UP HER MIND. She was going to brazen it out. Ma and Pa and Erlene were arriving Saturday and that was that. No doubt there were rooms to be had, or a house nearby. She'd just have to hoard her crab money to pay for it.

Gage was a matter of the heart. She had to convince him of her love. He didn't like gall. For him she'd purge every drop. The Bible said "the meek shall inherit the earth." If the Good Book said it was so, she reckoned she'd take a stab at it.

Gage was acting like a grizzly with a toothache, which had the effect of making meek more difficult to come up with than anger.

"If you tie it like that, you'll lose the float. Then you won't know where the traps are. This time, pay attention." He demonstrated an anchor knot for the third time.

Phoebe tied the knot. "When you have time I want you to show me how to tie a hangman's knot. I might find a use for it."

He glowered at her. "You want to trade tit for tat, or learn to crab?"

"Crab." She moved to the next trap and attached the float. Gage towered over her like an angry giant. She completed the task on the remaining traps. "Now what?"

"You missed one."

"That's thirteen. It's bad luck."

"It's stupid. Crabbing is crabbing, the more traps you have—"

"Bad luck is bad luck. I ain't courtin' it. Can I ask you a personal question?"

"You're going to ask it whether I permit it or not."

"Are you constipated? Bein' stopped up can cause a body to be in fearful moods. I can make a really good castor oil—"

Gage closed his eyes and ground out an obscene word.

"That's exactly what castor oil will make you do."

"I'm not in a mood!"

Phoebe expelled a disconsolate sniff. "Where's the bait? I got a notion somebody miswrote a passage in the Bible. I want to get out on the water and ponder on it."

The five gallon tub of crab bait smelled worse than dead crabs.

"You mean to tell me you paid good money for that slop?"

"It's called chum. You want to catch crabs or not?" Gage scooped up a can of chum and dropped it into the bait pocket. "Think you can manage from here on out?"

Phoebe allowed that she could. Dorie couldn't be pried from the chicks, Maydean from staring at her reflection, so Willie-Boy accompanied her in the boat. Gage had scrounged up some musty straw hats, and these they wore against the glimmer of bright sun on the water.

He watched her push away from the shore. "Remember what I said. When you set a trap, just throttle back on the motor, you don't have to shut it off."

"I reckon I know about motors. It can't be much different from driving a truck."

"This is exciting, ain't it Phoebe."

"Keep still Willie-Boy. You'll turn us over." It was a flat-bottomed skiff and sturdy, but Phoebe was taking no chances. She'd never ridden in a boat before. One hand on the throttle, she turned back to wave at Gage and met his astringent gaze. The boat somehow got off direction and nosed hard into the opposite bank. Phoebe jolted forward, knocking one of the traps into the water.

"Watch where you're going!" he yelled. Phoebe hauled the trap back aboard, grabbed a paddle and pushed away from the shore. She tried the throttle, getting the feel for the rudder. Now she had the hang of it. She could feel Gage's eyes on her still.

"You can swim, can't you?"

She had had meek up to her eyeballs. She only wanted the junkyard and its owner, not the entire earth. "No, but when I get back you can teach me how to walk on water!"

"Your face is bleedin', Phoebe. If we sink, the sharks will eat you."

She swiped at the scratch on her face with the tail of her shirt. "Face forward Willie-Boy, a shark ain't gonna stop me now."

It was thrilling being in charge of her fate again, being in business for herself—the right way. It took four trips to set out all the traps along the outer strip of marsh that separated the canal from the bayou. Each time she dropped a trap overboard Phoebe waited breathlessly for the marker float to come bobbing up. Each did. She could almost feel the crisp dollars that Hank would count into her hand.

When she cut the motor, stepped out and dragged the anchor deep on land she felt life was wonderful again.

She still needed gas for the truck, but now she knew where some was; in the five-gallon can that Gage kept for the lawn mower. She poured half of it into the truck and ran the motor a few minutes.

She walked down to the crab house to make sure Hank was buying crabs the next morning. He was. *Got all my ducks in a row this time,* Phoebe thought.

Essie called to her from the picking room. Phoebe sidestepped Stout before the supervisor could stop her.

"The church is sponsoring a trip to Bellingrath Gardens for the kids tomorrow. They have to bring their own lunch. You want yours to go? I can tell the bus driver to pick them up."

"I don't have to tag along?"

"No, that's the wonderful part. Sunday school teachers are takin' 'em. Ten to about three in the afternoon."

"I wouldn't mind gettin' the hellions off my hands for a few hours," Phoebe agreed.

"So you can have that hunk all to yourself?" Essie said slyly.

"What hunk?"

"Gage Morgan."

The seafood house wasn't sacred ground. "We're distant cousins."

"He wouldn't answer any questions about you, either," purred Essie.

"You didn't pry when I worked with you. How come you're doin' it now?"

"I never got the chance before. Work, work work, that's all you had a mind to do. He's prime ain't he?"

"Are folks talkin'?"

"Not so's you'd notice. They're watching, though. Especially since he brought you to church, and in Velma's car."

"Velma's dead."

"Ain't she though." Essie grinned.

"That's enough," announced Stout. "Essie, you here to pick or gab?"

Essie went back to work. Phoebe walked home, fierce determination in every step. Hawleys had always had an upstanding reputation. Phoebe shuddered to think what Ma would say if she arrived and got wind of such sly innuendo. Ma never did think it was her own who had a failing; what she'd have to say she'd say to Gage and ruin everything. Not that she was thinking bad about Ma, who loved her. No, it was just—Ma was Ma.

At the entrance to the yard Phoebe stopped and inspected her domain. One of these days she was going to coax Gage to move all the junk away from the path that led to the house. The grass around the homestead, now that it could accept sunshine, was turning green. The fence still leaned and the few slats that Willie-Boy had painted stood out like sore thumbs. It was time, Phoebe decided, that Gage knew just how helpful she could be outside of cooking and cleaning.

"This afternoon," she told the children after lunch, "we're gonna fix the fence, then paint it and the front porch."

Willie-Boy was offended. "I already painted the fence. Mr. Gage said I did a fine job."

"You did Willie-Boy, as far as you went, but it needs a second coat."

"I can't work in the sun. It's bad for my complexion. I don't want to end up freckled like you."

"Freckles don't ruin the texture of skin, Maydean, but Brillo pads do. Which is what it'll take to clean yours if you keep lathering on all that gunk. Dorie, you got any objections?"

"Can my chicks play in the front yard and keep me company?"

Phoebe nodded. "Now, if you kids work good, you'll not only have fifty cents, but tomorrow I'll let you go on a field trip with your Sunday school classes."

"A whole day away from you? I'll do it," piped Maydean. "If you'll let me wear mascara. All the other girls—"

"Ain't Hawleys. Fifty cents and the trip, or you can stay home and help me wash windows. That's my final word. Get your hat, Willie-Boy, you can show me where Gage keeps the paint."

"I'll have to wear my hat tomorrow, too. My gum patch ain't growed out."

It was a hot, sweaty, productive and glorious afternoon. The fence stood straight, each slat gleaming white; the porch railings got white paint and its floor glistened green. Phoebe sent the kids to wash up while she went to get Gage. She helloed from the entrance to the shop lest he accuse her of sneaking again.

"Am I disturbing you?"

"You are."

"I got my crab traps out."

"I know."

"Me and the kids fixed the fence and painted the porch."

"You didn't have to do that."

"It looks nice."

"I'm sure it does."

"You're actin' more grudgin' than Maydean."

He set aside a huge wrench, picked up another and inspected it. "You're trying to obligate me to you, Phoebe. I'm not going to let it happen."

"I ain't! I just wanted to do something nice. You've been good to us—to me. Better than any—"

He held up his hand. "I don't want to hear it. Cleaning, cooking, painting..." He made it sound like a crime. "You're trying to worm your way into my life."

"You're comparin' me to a worm?"

"It's just a figure of speech."

"I ain't no figure of speech. I'm a person. You didn't think I was no figure of speech the other night. You didn't—"

In one swoop he tossed aside the wrench, grasped Phoebe by her shoulders and shook her, not ungently. "Hush, damn it. I'm not trying to hurt your feelings. You have your life and I have mine. They don't dovetail. That's all I'm trying to say." Her freckles were subdued by a healthy red-brown tan. The straw hat framed her face, paint spatters and a small scratch gave it a gamin quality. The urge to absorb her, to take her surged through Gage. He felt her trembling. He dropped his hands to his sides. "The truth is I've never met anyone like you."

Phoebe marshalled her pride. "That's your bad luck."

Gage shook his head as if he'd suddenly lost track of their conversation. Every sharp word to Phoebe had sputtered and backfired. "You have a point."

She caught the subtle change in his tone and eyed him warily. "You're not mad anymore?"

"Only at myself. Come on, show me what you've been up to so I can be suitably appreciative."

"It looks real good from the road," Phoebe said as Gage inspected the improvements.

"So good it'll shame me into painting the rest of the house and maybe even the cash shack up at the gate."

"Sometimes people own a thing, and get so used to it they don't know what they've got." She sighed wistfully. "You've got a whole world here, Gage. A whole world."

"And you'd like to get your grubby little hands on it, wouldn't you?"

It was a neatly baited hook. Phoebe cruised around it. "I don't covet. The Bible speaks against it. I only said what I did because you let it run down and it goes against my nature to see a thing wasted. Dorie did her share, in case you want to make mention of it."

"I don't know if I can bear up under all these lessons in child rearing I'm getting."

"You're a good father," Phoebe said earnestly. "Like as not you'd do well to have three, four more."

His diaphragm seemed suddenly to swell, choking off his windpipe. "Back to work for me," he croaked.

Phoebe fanned her face with the brim of the old straw hat. "I'll send Willie-Boy to call you for supper."

PAINT, POLISH AND SOPHISTICATION never had been Phoebe's long suit and she knew it. But she was willing to use any magic, acquired or bought that would swing Gage around to her way of thinking.

Once the house was quiet she slipped into Dorie's room and dragged from beneath the bed the shoe box full of cosmetics and scents. Behind the locked bathroom door she pawed through it. Eye shadow made her look as if she'd run into a door; she scrubbed it off. Mascara made her eyes sting. She tried a bit of glossy lipstick, which made her lower lip appear set in a permanent pout. Not the image she wanted to present to

Gage. She found a vial of Wild Flower Musk and tried a drop on her wrist. It made her smell better than soap. Satisfied, she put some on her neck.

She returned the box to Dorie's room and tiptoed back to her own. She sat in the dark and waited for the line of light beneath Gage's door to go out. When it did, she counted to five hundred. She didn't want him to be wide awake.

She got as far as the foot of his bed. The lamp snapped on.

"Out!"

"I just want to talk."

Eyeing her with the wariness of a cornered fox, he adjusted a pillow against the headboard and leaned into it. "About what?"

"I'm embarrassed to say." She sat on the foot of the bed.

"You haven't been embarrassed since you were two days old. But if it makes you uncomfortable to say, why don't you just keep it to yourself?"

Phoebe picked at the sheet that lay over his shinbone. "Remember the other night?"

He did. "My mind's blank."

"I do all right in the daytime, because I keep busy. But as soon as it gets dark I start thinkin' about it. I can't *stop* thinkin' about it." She let her hand fall in the area of his knee. "Gage, I get so airy. If I was a balloon, I'd burst. Did you notice at supper? I could hardly swallow for—"

"You're worried about your appetite?"

Phoebe lowered her lashes. This wasn't going at all the way she planned. "I can go without food for days on end."

"Good, that'll save on groceries."

"Why're you making this so hard for me! Okay. You want me to eat crow? I'm here to eat crow. Can I get under the covers?"

"No."

"I'm taking off my nightgown."

"Don't do that."

Phoebe eyed the sheet at the juncture of his thighs. She thought she discerned a bit of activity there. She let her hand slide from his knee to the inside of his thigh. "Don't you remember how good it felt?"

"If we keep on we're going to be in over our heads— emotionally."

"I won't be in over my head. I know what I want. I want to do it again." Out of the corner of her eye Phoebe saw the sheet rise. Pretending her hand was an alien appendage over which she had no control she drew wider and wider circles with a fingertip on his thigh. Her hand brushed a most necessary part of his anatomy.

The cords on his neck stood out. "Stop teasing me."

She scooted up on the bed, picked up his hand, traced the calluses, then pressed his hand to her cheek. "I want you so much. Tell me you don't want me the same way. Make your tallywhacker go down."

He tried to laugh and failed. "I can't, damn it. You know I can't. You're a witch. Sex is new to you. I want you to think about when the magic wears off. What happens if you find someone you like better? Or—"

Phoebe paled. "You gotta quit comparin' me with you-know-who. Besides, I ain't gettin' naked for anybody else. It took all the gumption I had to do it with you."

Gage broke down and let her in. "Who wins against you?" He slid his hand behind her neck and pulled her to him. Phoebe's heart pounded and her breath sighed past his ear. He enclosed her in his arms and held her, not moving for long minutes. "You sound so convincing," he said despairingly and buried his face in her hair.

Phoebe's arms crept up around his neck. She lifted her face, her lips hovering above his so their breaths mingled. "Will you kiss me? Put your tongue in my mouth like you did the other night?"

Her lips parted and he tasted her sweet mouth, his tongue explored, thrust against hers. Phoebe sucked. He gasped. His arms tightened, then his hand began to travel; he slid her gown up and she felt his questing hand begin to roam over her flesh, felt his hand seek out and touch the pulsating flesh that made her woman. "Gage!" she whispered, shocked.

"Just giving you an idea of what you've put me through."

A shiver meandered down her spine. "I like it." Her voice was barely audible.

Gage snapped off the bed lamp. "Let's see what else we can do that you like."

"And then it'll be my turn?" Her voice was hoarse.

"And then it'll be your turn."

PHOEBE STRETCHED AND PURRED. "I'm learnin' so much about love."

"So am I," said Gage. He was half asleep.

"You know everything, you've been married. Imagine being able to do it anytime you wanted. It'd be heaven."

"Being married doesn't guarantee a good sex life."

Phoebe accepted that as an admission of the weakness of his own marriage. She knew all she wanted to know about Velma now. She didn't want Gage dwelling on the bad aspects of marriage. She wanted to feel him out on the idea of marrying her, but she couldn't think of the right thing to say. Instead she nestled close and nibbled on his ear. "Have you noticed how much Dorie has got to likin' me? She likes Maydean and Willie-Boy, too. I'll bet she'll like Ma and Pa and Erlene a lot."

"Probably." Gage said drowsily.

Phoebe stopped nibbling. Probably. That wasn't exactly an invite. She was stumped. Coming right out and asking might get a resounding no. "Gage, do we have an understandin'?"

"Like how?"

"Between you and me?"

"I'm beginning to think so. Time will tell."

"How much time?"

"I don't know. I can't see into the future."

Phoebe could. She could see three days ahead to Saturday and her whole life falling apart again.

"I suppose we could have Ma and Pa and Erlene visit, couldn't we? Ma would want to meet the man I take up with permanent."

He adjusted his pillow, buried his face in it. "Oh? I have to pass muster now?" came to her muffled.

"You would. Don't worry. Ma would be pleased as punch to meet you. And then she could look for a house in Bayou La Batre." She waited for a response. None came. "Gage, are you asleep?"

"I'm trying," he mumbled.

Phoebe snuggled against his back.

"You're just gonna love all the Hawleys."

"Not if they want to talk all night."

"You want me to shut up?"

"That's the nicest suggestion you've made all evening."

"It ain't. We already did the nicest."

"I'm begging you . . ."

Phoebe curled an arm over his abdomen and let her hand trail down to cradle his manhood. "G'night."

Gage's drowsiness began to slough away. "Oh, damn."

12

"YOUR LUNCHES ARE BAGGED and on the table in the living room," said Phoebe. "Don't forget them."

"Where's our drink money?"

Phoebe passed out the quarters. "Fifty cents each. Don't lose it. Willie-Boy, you know what you're supposed to do?"

"Don't run. Don't fight. Don't get lost. Don't talk with my mouth full."

"Dorie?"

"Same thing."

"Maydean?"

"Watch the brats."

"Get nice or get back in your room."

Maydean flounced. "Be ladylike."

"Okay. Finish breakfast and wait on the front porch for the church bus. I got to harvest my crabs. Gage, you got anything you want to add?"

"You've just about covered the Constitution."

"Daddy, can we have another quarter?"

Gage dug out change and passed it around.

Phoebe's eyes narrowed to slits. "You give out money that easy without them earnin' it?"

"I'm not always the skinflint you make me out to be."

"Then I mean to renegotiate the price of bumpers."

"That's not negotiable. I've got a seventy-dollar dent."

Phoebe sniffed. "You've also got a five-cent brain." She grabbed her straw hat off the broom hook. "I'm goin' crabbin'."

Gage followed her down to the canal. "I'll go with you this morning."

Phoebe gave him a winsome smile. "You like me so much now you can't bear for me to be outta sight?"

"Just want to keep an eye on my investment."

"You come in two parts, Gage Morgan. Purse part and pants part. When I first started fallin' for you, I figured it out. Everything a woman wants in a man is below the belt. Howsomever, I want you to know, I'm different. There are parts of you above the belt that I find particularly interestin'."

"Phoebe, if you start talking nasty, you can go out on that bayou by yourself and you'll never get a crab trap in the boat because you won't have me to show you the knack. See those old apple crates? Put 'em in the boat. I'll get the bait. We'll replenish each trap after we dump it. Saves time."

"Are you gonna boss me?"

"I'm going to do my damnedest and hope it takes."

"You're the kind of man who wants to wear the pants in the family?"

"Don't sound so disheartened. Around you, I don't seem to be able to keep them up."

Phoebe's heart overflowed. She sat on the oar seat and faced him, enjoying looking at him, smiling. He guided the boat through the cut and into the bayou. In the far distance she could see shrimp boats that were specks on the horizon. Gulls squawked and fished. The surface of the water was calm and sun-painted. They had the bayou to themselves. "Gage?"

"What?"

"You know that feeling I was getting only after dark? I'm starting to get it in the daytime, too."

"No."

She slipped off the seat onto her knees and rested her elbows on his legs. "I could unzip your pants and play."

"I've got to drive this boat."

"Nobody's around."

"It's early yet."

"I've never done it in the daytime." Her hands crept to his inner thighs. "We could just touch each other. That's all." She could see acceptance overtaking reluctance in his expression, could feel the shape taking place beneath her hands. She pressed her fingertips against the growing bulge between his legs.

"Let's get your traps emptied first...."

"I don't think I can wait."

"Try."

"I'm tormented." She unzipped his jeans, caressed the enlarging length of him and gazed unashamed into his eyes. "You said we could do whatever I felt was natural. That nothing was bad."

"I'm possessed," Gage moaned, and turned the boat into the tall marsh grasses.

"GAGE!"

"I'm in the living room."

Phoebe emerged from the hall and stopped short. "Why're you lyin' on the sofa? Why ain't you workin'? I came back from sellin' my crabs and found a customer hangin' about the cash shack lookin' for somebody to pay." She laid a ten dollar bill on his desk.

"Don't come within ten feet of me, Phoebe. I'm only thirty-five. I'd like to make thirty-six."

"Sex affects you worse'n liquor, don't it?"

Gage crooked an elbow over his eyes. "It doesn't even compare. If it ever happens that I have the opportunity to introduce another virgin to sex, I hope lightning strikes me dead."

"You wouldn't have to hope for lightning. I'd kill you myself."

He lifted his elbow and looked at her. "I know your methods. Lightning would be more humane."

"I can't help it if I start feelin' all tingly."

Gage dropped his elbow, covered his eyes. "If somebody had told me two weeks ago that I'd be done in by ninety pounds of spice and spit, I'd've laughed in his face."

Phoebe bristled. "Laugh now, why don't you?"

"Takes all my strength just to breathe."

"I want you to get out of the habit of insultin' me. I'm a Hawley and I don't take to it. It makes me mad."

"That's another thing. Soon as I can, I'm changing your name to Morgan. Then I won't have to listen to Hawley pride, Hawley gumption and Hawley grit."

Goose bumps erupted along Phoebe's arms. "We're gonna get married? When?"

"When I recover. I don't want any of my friends to see me like this."

Phoebe knelt down on the floor beside the sofa. "Gage, you love me? Truly?"

"Tried not to. Had good reason not to. I've been battered, abused and cuckolded. You'd think I'd learned my lesson."

Phoebe dragged his arm off of his face. "Look at me."

His eyes opened.

"There ain't another man in the world that can hold a candle to you. By my lights you're the best husband a body could have. I love you more than anything. Anything!"

Her warm sweet breath cascaded over him. He lifted his head and kissed her gently. "That's the most intoxicating thing anyone's ever said to me," he murmured.

"To prove how much I love you, I'm going to keep my clothes on," Phoebe announced. "I won't go near your tallywhacker again until after dark."

"Wonder of wonders."

"Anyway," Phoebe said decorously. "We need to settle the business betwixt us. I don't want to go into marriage owin' you." She reached into the pocket of her jeans and pulled out a roll of bills. "Crab money." Her hand trembled slightly. "Gage, back home in the mills I had to work all week for this much money." She counted out sixty-six dollars and put it in his hand. The remainder of the cash, she shoved quickly back into her pocket. "To repair your truck. Now I can have my bumper and tag back."

"I was going to let you have it anyway."

Phoebe grinned. "I wouldn't've taken it. You're gonna have to live with Hawley pride right up to the minute I'm a Morgan."

Gage folded the bills and put them in his shirt pocket. "In that case, what's Hawley pride have to say about anteing up my share of crab money? I need a new suit to get married in."

Phoebe wondered if the time was ripe to tell him about Ma and Pa and Erlene's arriving on Saturday. A little voice in her head was saying, *You think you know what you're doing, Phoebe. You think you know how Gage will react. But you don't. You'd better be careful.*

She decided against it. Life was going her way for a change. She didn't want any by-chance interference.

"First debt owed is first debt I pay," she said. "Not to worry, I'll settle up with you fair and square on the crabbin'."

"I trust you." He smiled a smile that made her insides turn to lead. There was a whole world of meaning behind the words. The specter of Ma and Pa and Erlene thrust into her brain. But no. That's not what he meant. He meant adultery.

"I won't ever give you cause not to trust me," she said thickly. "I promise." Gripped by something stronger than passion and unable to voice it, she reached out and traced his mouth with a fingertip. "You sure do have kissin' lips...."

"Don't start talking sex," he pleaded, suffering a slow inexorable tightening of the nether regions of his body. "You have to learn that talking about it is erotic, at least to a man."

"It is?"

"Yes."

Phoebe sat back on her heels and demurely clasped her hands in her lap. "You mean if I just talked about what we did in the boat without even touching you, you'd—"

"Exactly."

"Lor!" Unexpected streams of excitement lazily uncoiled inside her. "Gage?"

"What?"

"Did you like the part where I unzipped your pants and played with—"

"I'm not listening."

"What about when I unbuttoned your shirt and sucked your nipples?"

"Be quiet!"

"What about . . ." Phoebe put her lips to his ear and whispered.

Gage reached out with an unsteady arm and encircled her. "I'm lost," he groaned.

"WHY IS DADDY IN BED so early? Is he sick?"

"He's just takin' a nap. Nothing's wrong with him a good sleep won't cure. Close that kitchen door so we don't wake him. I want to hear all about your day."

"I don't want to talk about mine," said Willie-Boy.

"You didn't have a good time?" Phoebe put platters of fried pork chops and potatoes on the table.

"I almost did. But a girl named Kimmie kept followin' me around. She even tried to kiss me. I thought I was gonna be sick."

"Maydean, why're you wearin' such a long face?"

"I can't enter the beauty contest."

"Who said?"

"One of the girls in my Sunday school class. You have to be a senior in high school." Her eyes filled with tears. "By then I'll be old and wrinkled."

"Pooh. By then you'll be even prettier."

Maydean eyed Phoebe warily. "Why're you saying such nice things to me?"

"I'm in a good mood. I sold my crabs and paid Gage off for our bumper and tag."

Maydean froze. "Are we gonna go home now?"

Willie-Boy's fork stopped at his mouth. "Are we gonna see Ma and Pa?"

Dorie's face crumbled. "Well, you can just leave then! The sooner the better!" The nine-year-old jumped from the table and raced out of the kitchen. Phoebe caught the door before it slammed.

"What's wrong with her?" Maydean said, scowling.

"If you'd look outside yourself once in a while, you'd know. We made her feel left out. You two eat, I'll go talk to her."

Dorie was sprawled face down with the pillow over her head. Phoebe sat on the edge of the bed.

"Go away!" came Dorie's muffled command.

"In a minute. I need to talk to you. I've got a secret. Howsomever, I can't tell you unless you swear not to tell."

Dorie lifted the pillow and peeked out. "A good secret?"

"You might not think so."

"What is it?" Dorie sat up against the headboard and hugged the pillow to her stomach.

"You have to swear not to tell, even if you don't like it."

The child hesitated, torn between sulking and curiosity. "Cross my heart," she finally said, doing it.

"First I have to ask you a question."

"Is the question part of the secret?"

"Sort of. What do you think about your pa?"

Dorie's interest dissolved. "He's all right. He's just my daddy."

"What do you think about him gettin' married?"

Dorie's face took on a troubled expression. "Could he?"

"If he wanted to, which he might."

"He's too old."

Phoebe opened her mouth to protest that, but changed her mind. "He is, and the older he gets the more likely he'll need someone to look after him. How would you feel about having a stepmother?"

"Would she boss me?"

"No more than I do."

"Did he tell you who she is?"

"I have a close acquaintance with her," Phoebe said. "She's about as good-hearted a person I know."

"Who is it?"

For once in her life, Phoebe's wealth of courage failed her. "That's the second part of the secret. I can't say until I'm sure you're gonna keep the first part."

Dorie suddenly appeared stricken. "Is it Belle Martin?"

Phoebe's eyes narrowed. "Who's Belle Martin?"

"She brought food every day after Momma died. She tried to kiss Daddy on his cheek."

"The brazen hussy! Gage wouldn't choose her coming or going!"

"Every time she looked at me she wrinkled her nose."

"If she ever wrinkles her nose at you again, you point her out to me. I'll break it for her."

Dorie smothered a giggle, then looked at Phoebe. "If you and Daddy didn't fuss so much, maybe he'd marry you."

Phoebe saw her chance, but she couldn't make herself jump all the way into it. "I could try to talk him into it," she said with a sigh, as if the idea of marrying Gage Morgan was little more than a daily chore. "But when I get married I want babies and I guess I'd worry about how you'd take that."

"Real babies?" Dorie's eyes grew wide.

"Real babies. Now that you've brought it up, though, if I married Gage, then Maydean would be your aunt by marriage and Willie-Boy would be your uncle."

"But Willie-Boy is littler than me!"

"See what I mean? Your Pa wouldn't like to do anything that'd make you unhappy."

"Willie-Boy's all right when he's not being a pest."

Phoebe assumed a properly sober expression. "Ain't he, though?"

Dorie displayed a sudden anxiety. "What do you think my momma would say?"

This was the all-important point. Phoebe shook her head. "It's hard to imagine, what with her bein' in heaven and all. My opinion is that she'd appreciate knowin' you were cared for. She loves you and people who love always want to see their loved ones happy."

"I'm happy with you and Maydean. But Belle doesn't make me happy. She scares me. Why don't you tell Daddy to marry you, Phoebe?"

"I'm not sure he'd take to the idea, as stubborn as he is."

"You could try."

"Tell you what. You come back to the table and finish your supper while I ponder on it. If it comes about and he mentions it to you, you'll have to appear surprised. Men don't like to think we women conspire behind their backs."

"You like me, don't you Phoebe?"

"Mostly," Phoebe replied, knowing that a child had keen insight and could see through pretense. "I'd like you a passel more if the next time you ran in here to sulk, you'd take your sandals off first. Now I got to wash this bedspread again."

"I COULDN'T'VE DONE a better job of it myself," Phoebe said, admiring the manner in which Gage had welded her bumper back onto the truck. She also admired the way his biceps tightened, the way his back muscles rippled. Her heart fluttered, but she restrained herself. "I reckon I'll go get it gassed up before we harvest crabs this morning."

"I'm not getting in that skiff with you. Take May-dean or Dorie."

"But I let you sleep all night and I didn't pester you before breakfast either."

"Lucky me."

Phoebe paid no attention to his doleful glare. "You're back to thinkin' I'm too skinny—"

"Nope, I'm thinking survival."

"Don't you want to do it even the least little bit?"

"I want to. . . ." Sweat began to bead on his upper lip. "But I have work to do."

"You're so strong-willed, Gage. I admire that in a man."

"Just so long as you admire from a distance."

"I can't promise." Phoebe thought about his body in her power and felt her insides begin to tremble. But the yard was open for business and the kids were running loose. Privacy was not assured. Practicality swayed her. The letter from Ma Hawley suddenly loomed large in her mind. "Anyway, I'm glad we got the truck fixed. It don't belong to me, you know. It's Pa's. I got to return it."

Gage wiped his hands on a rag, taking an inordinate amount of time doing it. "Don't think I want you going off anywhere. I'm feeling possessive."

"Oh. Well, what about if Pa came and got it?"

"That'd be better."

All of Phoebe's nerve endings began to hum. "Maybe Ma and Erlene could come down with Pa on the bus. Ma wouldn't countenance me getting married without her being there. She'd like to know it's so."

"That sounds reasonable. But Phoebe, don't go planning a big wedding."

"I thought just family."

He looked at her from beneath his thick sweep of dark lashes. "You're too agreeable, too fast. I get the feeling you're somehow putting something over on me."

"I'm agreeable because I'm so happy," she reassured with a grand air, gliding toward him, putting her hand on his arm. "Gage, let me kiss you. I won't put my tongue in your mouth and make you crazy. I just want to feel your lips on mine."

"You're dodging the issue. Just family," he mused, keeping his gaze hard on her. "How many aunts, uncles and cousins have you got back up in those hills?"

"There's just Ma and Pa and Erlene. Joey and his wife won't come because of the baby."

"I don't want to spend a lot of money on froufrous getting married."

"Me, either. I want us to save our money for solid things. And I aim to use my crab money for the particulars. We got to have a weddin' feast, but Ma and I can cook that. Ma can bake the cake. The only outsiders ought to be the preacher and his wife. It wouldn't be polite to slight them."

The questioning in his eyes faded, then brightened once again. "Just so there's no misunderstanding let's agree right now. I'll set aside four hundred dollars for us getting married outside of your ring. Not a penny more."

Four hundred dollars. Lor! She could get married ten times over for that. It descended on her with a shock that his idea of parsimony was far more generous than her own. "I'll make that do," she said solemnly. "I'll eke out every dime." She slid her hand up his arm. "Now, will you kiss me, or do you aim to make me suffer daylight to dusk?"

He bent his head and pressed his mouth lightly to hers. Phoebe nibbled on his lower lip.

"Stop that," he murmured even as his arms went about her, tightening his embrace. Phoebe pressed her thigh to his, felt the quicksilver stirring in his loins. She was aglow with feminine power. All would be well. Even when Ma and Pa arrived. She just knew it. Gage ended the kiss reluctantly.

Phoebe's heart was filled with tenderness. "Gage, I'm going to make you the best wife in the universe."

"You don't have to be the best, Phoebe. Just belong to me."

There was an underlying insistence in his voice. Phoebe stepped out of his arms. "God put you in my path, Gage. There was never a man before you and there won't be after. Married to you I'm going to be the envy of every woman between here and Mobile. I ain't givin' that up."

The deep dark cave that was his heart filled with warmth and light. "Get out of here and go crabbing before my willpower fails me," he said gruffly.

"Is it about to?" she asked hopefully.

"Mr. Gage!" Willie-Boy shouted as he hurried into the shop. "Did you get that bike fixed for me yet?"

"Reprieve," Gage muttered, grinning at Phoebe.

Phoebe tilted her head and returned his grin. "Wait until after dark."

13

"IT'S BEEN DARK for hours." Gage stood on the threshold of Phoebe's bedroom, peering in. "Isn't there some little promise or other you wanted to make good on?"

"I was waitin' for the kids to get hard asleep." She stretched sinuously, arching; the line of her throat was compellingly vulnerable. She was stopped for a moment by Gage's eyes riveted on her, then she smiled. For modesty's sake he wore pajama bottoms, but they did little to hide his aroused state. "Have you been layin' abed thinkin' of me?"

"I was reading the paper."

Phoebe laughed. She felt so bold. "Tell me one thing you read."

"I read my horoscope. It said for me not to tolerate any teasing." He crossed the room, scooped her into his arms. "It said I should be creative in an affair of the heart."

Cradled in his arms, Phoebe felt no more substantial than a willow. "What else did it say?" she asked weakly.

He nuzzled her neck as he carried her into his own room to place her on his bed. "It said I should drag you by the hair on your head into my lair and strip you naked." He took the hem of her gown, pulled it up. Phoebe's arms slid out.

"Did it say anything about closin' and lockin' the door to the lair?"

"Leave it to you to be the practical one. Good thing you don't write horoscopes."

"Good thing I'm here so you can make it come true."

His eyes, opaque with passion, took in her shoulders, the tidy mounds of her breasts. Small breasts, round with dainty nipples.

When he returned to the bed he lay down beside her, pressed his lips into the curve of her neck and began to stroke every inch of her.

His hot kisses distracting her, Phoebe couldn't keep track of where his hands were going, what they were doing. His hands, then his lips closed over her exposed breasts, and a pleased sound erupted from him as he pulled her against him, forcing her to feel him jutting against her thighs. He was making her body dance, flooding her with heat.

"Gage!" she cried, her voice small, vanishing as his tongue dipped into a most intimate crevice. He ignored her protests. Something extraordinary seemed to be happening inside her. Air escaped her lungs, blood seemed to suffuse her head, her muscles rippled as if they were separate entities borne haphazardly on a sudden wind; an unfamiliar interior fluttering seemed to warn her of something about to take place, some desperate event needing completing. A sensation, unlike anything she'd ever experienced pierced her brain, then radiated out until all of her being was seized, frozen. There was a tremendous swelling, a building pressure in her loins, and a startled cry broke from her throat as the immense feeling savagely exploded.

She was dying, separating into different selves, she could scarcely breathe. She felt all at once lighter.

As if attuned to the shuddering waves, Gage whispered, "Darling . . . finally . . ."

She wondered how he could know, feeling as if the secret was exposed, on display. She touched his face lightly, whispered his name.

He came up over her, kissing her breasts, her throat, her mouth so that she opened to his thrusting presence, captured by the hardness riding between her thighs. Whatever had happened inside her body seemed to have created in him a surging ardor, some higher level of stimulation. She gave herself up to him and closed her mind to all else.

"I THOUGHT I was dying," she said in an awed, ragged voice that was hers but not hers. Gage had tilted the lamp shade so that the circle of light was aimed outward and they lay within only softly lit shadows. Phoebe risked a look at him. His eyes were narrowed, he was smiling at her. "Somethin's funny?"

"Nope. I'm happy. Would you rather I frowned?"

"You don't look happy. You look smug. Do you know what happened to me?"

"Sure do."

She let her gaze wander over his face, reading every nuance of his expression, searching for truth. "Does it happen to you? Every time?"

"Sure does."

"I don't think I could bear it again."

"Oh? That's too bad. Most women suffer themselves to get used to it."

"Most women? What most women?"

"Tell you what. I'll buy twin beds for after we're married. That way you won't be tempted."

"But I like bein' in bed with you. I like—I ain't spendin' my whole married life in separate beds. Anyway, it just took me by surprise. I didn't know there was more than . . . than what I'd already felt."

"What's the solution then? I don't want to force you to do something you find unbearable." As if the subject were finished, he lifted her hand and inspected her ring finger. "Remind me, I'll measure this with a string tomorrow."

"I could get used to it."

"I don't want to buy something that doesn't fit."

"I didn't think I was really goin' to die."

"White gold, I think."

Phoebe jerked her hand from his. "Pay attention!"

"Attention? Oh, you mean like this?" He secured her body to his with a powerful arm, savoring the prominence of her pelvic bones pressed to his.

"I'm thinkin' I could probably bear it if it happened again."

He played with her body, probed and kissed and caressed her, offering her pleasure, torture. "Just tell me if it gets to be unbearable and I'll stop."

"If you stop," Phoebe said breathlessly, "I'll go out and buy those twin beds myself."

UP UNTIL FRIDAY AFTERNOON Phoebe felt she was dangling on a string from heaven. The crab catches continued to be profitable. She'd divided with Gage, and still she had a hundred dollars. It was more money than she'd ever had left over at the end of a week. She kept going into her room and reaching beneath the pillow for her purse just to take the bills out and count them.

She hadn't yet mentioned the imminent arrival of the remaining members of her family. Ma would be expecting to live in Gage's house, but Phoebe could see now that wasn't going to work. She and Gage hardly had privacy to snatch a stolen kiss during the day as it was. With Ma and Pa and Erlene underfoot, even nights would be impossible. Especially with Erlene, who had a tendency to wander. Still, Ma couldn't take care of Erlene and Pa and Maydean and Willie-Boy by herself. The dilemma preyed on her mind.

Maybe, she thought, Vinnie would begrudge the bus fare and decide Ma and Pa could stay on. It was a dim hope, but that at least would give Phoebe time to sort it all out. Time to put by enough money to get Ma started in her own place, one close enough that Phoebe could be of help. She wished Vinnie and Joey had a telephone. She'd go this minute and call and tell Ma to stay put. But they didn't and all that was left to her was to get the house ready, and to tell Gage.

But no matter how she practiced the words in her mind, in his presence they refused to be uttered. She was caught hopelessly in the undertow of love, wanting to do nothing to jeopardize the happiness of the moment.

"I have the urge to step out tonight," Gage said when he came into the house for a glass of ice water.

"I don't hold with a man goin' out and leavin' his intended long-jawed and mopin'."

"Long-jawed and moping." Gage laughed. "I don't think I hold with it myself. Anyhow, I don't dare leave you alone. You might find some other man to drive out of his mind. What do you say we go into Mobile, treat the kids to a movie while we window shop?"

"After supper?"

"Let's just make an evening of it. Eat at McDonald's. Dorie likes hamburgers and I want to soften her up before I mention getting married."

"I imagine she'll take it okay. She likes me. She likes Maydean and Willie-Boy. And I just know she's going to like Ma and Pa and Erlene."

"Dorie does seem to stay in Maydean's pocket, so to speak. I guess it's good for her. I wouldn't mind if Willie-Boy and Maydean finished out the summer with us."

"You wouldn't?"

"If your folks don't mind."

"I don't think they'll mind. As a matter of fact..." Her hand fluttered as if to erase her unspoken thought.

Gage had the impression that Phoebe was concentrating hard on the moment while another part of her was staring into something of such compelling importance it couldn't be ignored. A personal vision, zealously guarded. He waited for her to go on, but when she didn't he said, "As a matter of fact, what?"

"Oh, nothing. I'd better get the clothes off the line, round up everybody. What time do you want us ready?"

"About five."

When she came out of the laundry room with the empty clothes basket he stopped her. "Phoebe, what's on your mind?"

"Gettin' the clothes folded and put away."

"Look, we're going to be learning things about each other the rest of our lives. At least, I hope we are. But one thing we have to have from the start is trust. So why don't you trust me with whatever is bothering you."

Phoebe exhaled. "Nothin's botherin' me. I'm just a worrier is all."

Her tone was tense. She was lying. He knew it. But he could see she'd stick to her guns. "Are you having second thoughts about getting married? About me? Was I too rough last—"

Phoebe threw her arms around him and pressed her face into his chest. "I love you more than myself. I don't want to lose you. I don't want anythin' to happen—"

"Is that all? You're not going to lose me—unless you beat me to death with that clothes bask—"

"Are y'all kissin'?"

They jerked apart. "Where'd you come from, Willie-Boy?"

"Nowhere. Were you trying to kiss Phoebe? BoBo Gardner tried to kiss her once and she threw a pot of beans on him."

"I hope I don't suffer the same fate."

"I got work to do," said Phoebe. "Willie-Boy, you find Dorie and Maydean. Gage is treatin' all of you to a movie."

Willie-Boy turned pale. "No!"

Gage laughed. "Yes."

"I only been to a movie once and I was too little to remember." He sprawled on the porch. "I've got to lay down here and savor my good fortune."

"Savor your good fortune?" Gage repeated. "That's a mouthful."

"That's what Pa says. He sets in his rocking chair and savors his good fortune."

"What else does your dad do?"

"What Ma tells him to."

Smiling, Gage walked away from that with the sense that Hawley women liked to rule the roost. But no woman would ever again rule the Morgan roost. He had turned loose the reins once only to end up a cuckolded, widowed fool. He'd never allow it again. With Phoebe his dignity had been recouped. He meant to keep it intact.

THE SHOPPING MALL proved to be an adventure in prudence and self-control. Phoebe held tightly to her purseful of money against every lure and inducement.

There were candy shops, ice-cream parlors, dress shops, gold shops, shoe shops, toy shops, beauty shops, pet stores, book stores, and department stores with counter after counter of cosmetics from which they had to drag Maydean. McDonald's was at one end of the mall, the movie theater at the other. Gage bought the movie tickets and passed out cash for popcorn and soft drinks.

"Those kids are gonna be sick," warned Phoebe. Willie-Boy was so excited she feared an attack of asthma.

"I'll do my breathing exercises, I promise," he wailed.

"I'll take care of him," insisted Dorie.

Phoebe gave in, but waited outside the theater ten minutes on the chance he'd swoon and have to be carried out.

"I'm going to Sears to pick out a suit," Gage said.

"I'll come with you."

"No you won't. I like to buy my own clothes. I'll meet you back here in an hour."

The beauty shop lured Phoebe like a magnet. She stood outside and watched men and women coming out looking groomed and happy. Not a frowner in the bunch. She had her hair cut in the manner suggested by the stylist. She walked out of the shop with her curls tamed and hugging her head. She stopped in front of every display window admiring her reflection. Tilting her head this way and that until a sales clerk came out and asked did she want to try it on.

"What?"

"The dress. It's made for you."

Phoebe refocused her attention beyond her own reflection. The outfit was the most exquisite she'd ever seen. A lacy cream colored blouse tucked into a skirt beneath which peeked a matching slip trimmed in eyelet. She saw herself in the dress standing next to Gage in front of the preacher. "How much is it?"

"Why don't you try it on," the saleslady coaxed. "It's on sale."

"I like a bargain," said Phoebe. The lace on the blouse draped her shoulders and enhanced her slender neck. The sale price was fifty-nine dollars plus tax. Heart thudding and feeling faint Phoebe parted with the money—more money than she'd ever spent on a single garment in her life. She went back to the bench in front of the theater, waited for Gage, closed her eyes and prayed for the next morning to produce the best crab catch in existence.

"Phoebe! What've you done to your hair?"

"Had it tamed."

"You sure did."

"You don't like it?"

"I like it fine. It makes you look . . . elegant."

Phoebe's eyes burned with pleasure, but her mouth turned down at the corners. "I bought my wedding dress."

"Don't sound so terrible about it. Let me see."

"Can't. That's bad luck. Anyway, I might want to take it back. Did you get a suit?"

"I got fitted for one. Come on. Let's browse—"

"I ain't movin' off this bench." She had twenty-one dollars left to her name and she was determined not to be parted from another dime. She had three good reasons in the back of her mind why she should return at once to the dress shop and get her money back. They were Ma, Pa and Erlene.

"You're the unhappiest bride-to-be I've ever seen," Gage accused.

Phoebe forced her most winning smile. "I'm just nervous. I ain't never been married before."

Gage put his arm around her and drew her close. "It's not going to be much different from the way we're living now."

Oh, yes it is, thought Phoebe.

DEEP INTO THE NIGHT Phoebe made love to Gage with an uncommon frenzy. She kissed his toes, his knees, explored every line and tendon of his body as if driven by necessity to commit the whole of him to memory.

At one point he took her hands into his, halting her. "Darling, we have an entire lifetime."

"Promise you'll love me no matter what."

"The vows go 'for better or for worse.'"

"Suppose with me it's worse."

"With you my life is nothing but better. Speaking of which, some things are better done slowly. Lie back. Loving you is one of them."

AT BREAKFAST Gage made the announcement. "What do you kids think? Phoebe and I are going to be married."

Maydean was speechless.

Willie-Boy said, "Does that mean you won't have time to teach me to ride my bike today?"

Dorie cut a conspirator's glance at Phoebe. "That's nice, Daddy. Maydean's gonna be my aunt."

Gage leaned back in his chair. "I don't know why, but I did expect some banshee yelling—"

Phoebe couldn't put it off another minute. "And Ma and Pa and Erlene are coming." It felt so good to finally get the words out she sagged against the sink counter.

"When?" yelled Willie-Boy. "Oh, I miss Ma!"

"I don't know yet," said Phoebe, which was the truth, because she hadn't yet called the Greyhound bus station for the time the bus from Cottontown arrived.

Maydean found her tongue, directing her question to Gage. "It's okay with you if Ma and Pa and Erlene come?"

"It's fine. I want to meet them. And if you and Willie-Boy want, you can stay with Phoebe and myself until school starts."

"I never want to leave," said Willie-Boy. "Ma won't either when she sees—"

"Willie-Boy!" Phoebe interrupted. "You can help me harvest crabs this mornin'."

Dorie got up and went to stand at her father's elbow. "Phoebe said she'd get me a real baby."

"I'm goin' crabbin' now!" Phoebe grabbed her hat with one hand, Willie-Boy with the other.

Gage was out the door on her heels. "Get the chicks some water, Willie-Boy, I want to have a private word with your sister. A real baby, eh?" he said to Phoebe after the boy made himself scarce.

"By 'n' by, is what I meant."

"Is it? You and Dorie must've had a nice little chat."

"I didn't want to get my heart set on you and then have Dorie dragging about unhappy."

"You stole my thunder."

"I didn't know you wanted to do the tellin'."

"I'm the head of this house."

"Bein' partners is better."

"Okay, but I'm the head of this partnership. If it happens there's any news such as any more little Morgans, I want to be the first to know."

"You will be."

"Have you got anything else up your sleeve?"

"Lor! What makes you say that?"

"Your chin's coming at me."

"Can't think of anythin'."

"I'm not a man who likes surprises, Phoebe. They're never in my favor."

"I'll remember," Phoebe said and sat down on the stoop to tie her shoelaces.

"Well, since we're officially engaged, I'm going to make you a present of the crab business."

Phoebe kept sitting, she didn't trust herself to stand. "You are?" She could see herself getting rich on her own account. "First thing I'm gonna do is buy you a wedding ring."

"To match the one you've put in my nose? No thank you. Can't wear rings doing the work I do."

"What can I give you then?"

"What you've been giving me. Yourself."

Phoebe tilted her head and lowered her lashes. "You want to go crabbin' with me this mornin'?"

"No more boat gymnastics. You're trying to put me on crutches."

"We can just—"

"No. You've moved into my brain as it is. My body can't keep up. Now, go harvest your crabs before I end up in a wheelchair." He started to walk away, then turned. "What I'm looking forward to...is going to bed with you, waking up with you. I never had that with Velma. She wanted the romance, but not—"

"Gage? Is Velma going to be living with us?"

He shook his head. "No. She's gone. It's just you and me, and Dorie."

And Ma and Pa and Erlene and Maydean and Willie-Boy, thought Phoebe. *And dear heavenly Father, what am I going to do?*

As soon as she returned from selling her crabs, Phoebe called the Greyhound bus station. No buses came to Bayou La Batre. The bus station was in Mobile and the bus from Cottontown was expected at four forty-five.

After putting it off and putting it off, at three-thirty she went out to the gate shack. Between helping customers, Gage was teaching Willie-Boy how to ride the bicycle he'd put together.

"I want to go into Mobile," she said.

"Shopping again?"

"I just want to go."

"For what?"

"Will you keep an eye on the kids?"

"What's the mystery?"

"It's no mystery to me. I just want to go by myself." She could explain everything to Ma, so Ma wouldn't be expecting to live under the same roof.

Gage gave her a puzzled look, then locked the gate shack. "Let's go talk about this. You've been acting funny."

They sat on the porch. Phoebe's eyes were glued fearfully to his.

"Spill it," he said.

"It's Ma and Pa and Erlene. They're comin'."

"I know that."

"But you said you didn't like surprises."

"I'm not surprised. We discussed it."

"They're comin' *today*."

"You called them?"

Phoebe hesitated. "Do you mind?"

"I don't mind their coming. I mind your not telling me you called."

"How mad are you gonna get?"

He retreated into himself for a few moments. "Don't guess I'll get mad at all."

"Gage! Truly?"

He grimaced. "Now I'm nervous. Meeting prospective in-laws . . ."

"Their bus gets in this afternoon. You can stay here. I'll take Willie-Boy—"

"I wouldn't think of it. I'll go with you to pick them up. We'll take the car."

"But—"

"No buts. I'll get a shower." He put his arm around her. "One thing I won't forgive you for . . . had I known we'd have a houseful tonight, I'd've taken you up on that offer you made me this morning."

She was powerfully aware of his arm about her. Powerfully aware of the delicacy of the situation. "You're certain we're gonna get married no matter what? I don't want to introduce you to Ma as my intended, then have to take it back."

"We'll set it up with the pastor tomorrow after church. How's that for positive?"

Phoebe looked out over the yard. Willie-Boy was on his bike. Maydean and Dorie were playing drive-in in the old car. Ma and Pa and Erlene were assured a fine welcome. First thing Monday, she'd take her crab money and find them a place to live. All was so good with her world, she was beside herself.

"Gage?" She put her hand on his knee, trailed it slowly up the inside of his thigh. "Can I wash your back?"

WILLIE-BOY WAS THE FIRST to spot his parents. Ma Hawley smothered him in hugs. "Oh, I've missed my best boy!"

Phoebe felt suddenly shy at introducing Gage. "Ma, this is the man I told you about. We're gonna get married. That's why he wanted you to come. Gage, this is

Ma. I reckon you can call her Annabelle. That's my pa, Elmo, and that's Erlene."

"You're Phoebe, aren't you?" Erlene said as Gage shook hands all around.

"That's right."

"I remembered."

Phoebe kept a weather eye on Gage as he took in her family. He couldn't miss Pa's walking sticks or Erlene's childlike demeanor. Ma was shooting her questioning looks, but Phoebe gave an imperceptible shake of her head.

Luggage was gathered, Erlene guided and Pa directed. Willie-Boy filled in the conversational gaps telling about the junkyard, his bike, his welding career, and the terrible girl, Kimmie, who had tried to kiss him.

"Have I ever been in a car before?" asked Erlene.

"'Course you have," Phoebe told her. She caught Gage glancing at Erlene in the rearview mirror. His expression was inscrutable.

"I brought my knee pads," said Elmo. "I mean to get in a winter garden. You said the land was fair rich?"

"We already got potato hills in," said Phoebe. "You don't have to put in a garden for us, Pa. I'll do that."

"I want to," said Elmo. "I like to make myself useful."

Phoebe smiled over Willie-Boy's head at Gage. "Hawleys can't sit still for a minute." Then to avoid any slips of tongue Phoebe plied question after question about Joey, Vinnie, the baby, neighbors. She talked of Maydean, Dorie, crabbing.

"I wasn't expectin' to find you set up with a man," Annabelle said in the second Phoebe was trying to think up another conversational gambit.

"Oh, Ma! You like to joke. Gage thinks I have wit, too. He said so. I promised you'd bake the weddin' cake."

"Reckon I will, if you have the ingredients."

Phoebe was hoarse by the time Gage halted the car in front of the house. "Lor!" exclaimed Annabelle, eyeing him with respect. "Phoebe girl, you done good."

"There's Dorie and Maydean. Ma look at Maydean. She's gettin' prettier. And this is Gage's daughter, Dorie."

"I woulda knowed her anywheres by the way you described her in your letter," said Annabelle.

"On the telephone, Ma. I told you about Dorie on the telephone. This mornin', when I called you."

"Telephone? But—oh, my, yes." Annabelle went on quickly and smiled lopsided at Gage. "I'm gettin' so I disremember about as bad as Erlene."

Gage took in the elderly woman, her red fussy face, the old man, stooped, maneuvering painfully on his canes and Erlene who had an innocence more profound than that of his own nine-year-old daughter. His gaze shifted to Phoebe. Her gamin face, framed now so innocently by the halo of curls, was a picture of guilt and duplicity. He'd been conned. The whole of the past two weeks had been nothing more than a hoax. Love, sex, joy. The good feelings. All a trick. All that he admired in Phoebe, her singlemindedness, had been aimed at one goal: to find a place for her family. He'd been duped into offering his own. Gorge rose up in his throat.

"I'll leave Phoebe to get all of you settled," he said with stiff civility.

"Why, certain. We'll just make ourselves at home."

"I'm sure you will."

His tone, the pasted-on smile sent a shiver of alarm racing down Phoebe's spine. She trailed him out onto the porch. "Where you goin', Gage?"

"We'll talk later," he said, looking hard into her eyes.

It was a warning. She felt the weight of reality crushing down on her. "You said they could come!"

"I guess I just wanted to believe in magic, in fairy tales. You conned me from the instant we met. That letter you wrote the first day you were here . . . There wasn't any job. It was to tell your parents you'd found a sucker, wasn't it?"

"I can make you understand." She put her hand on his arm. He jerked away.

"It hurts, Phoebe. I didn't know it could hurt so much. First Velma, now you . . ." He shook his head. "Being disillusioned twice in one lifetime is once too much for me."

She wanted to follow him to the car, plead with him to allow her to explain. She wanted to grasp his arm, keep him from leaving, but Erlene was trying to march past her and Ma was calling her, exclaiming over the size of the house, the television, insisting Phoebe show her the bedrooms, the kitchen.

Gage didn't show up for supper. Phoebe sorted out the sleeping arrangements, which left her the sofa . . . or Gage's bed. But she didn't dare sleep there. She lay stiffly on the sofa, waiting, listening to night sounds— the occasional squawk of a gull, the muted chorus of crickets—listening for the sound of Gage's car.

GAGE DREW UP on the point that overlooked the bay. God had played a joke on him, he thought. He'd been vulnerable. He could see that now. Like all strong people, he'd taken his loneliness in stride—until Phoebe had burst upon his household . . . his heart.

Phoebe had homed in on his vulnerability, and like a fool he'd just lapped up all the attention she'd bestowed on him. But now she'd filled his house with her family, and he knew unerringly that that had been her goal from the moment she'd set foot on his property. And stupid as he was, he'd gone and left it to them.

By damn, he'd go back. He'd. . . No, he couldn't turn them out. He leaned his head against the door frame and closed his eyes. Visions of Phoebe leaped into his mind's eye. He would let them stay. Maybe they'd soothe some of the pain in him.

He would rest a bit, he thought. Rest, think and plan. Then he'd go back to the house and give Phoebe all the misery she deserved.

He would let her fuss and fume until she was dangling at the end of her precious pride. He'd show her how it felt to be a victim.

THE SUN CAME UP on a morning full of promise. Phoebe didn't have eyes for the beauty of it.

Ma Hawley had church on her mind. Phoebe pleaded a headache and watched her family drive out of the yard. Dorie sat between Ma and Pa to guide the way. Maydean, Erlene and Willie-Boy sat cross-legged in the truckbed on a blanket to protect their Sunday clothes.

Phoebe couldn't face the disappointment of church; Gage had promised to speak to the preacher. She supposed now that whatever Christian spirit she'd resurrected in him had shrunk to nothingness. She had that cross of sin to bear. She had a terrible emptiness inside. She couldn't decipher which hurt the most.

She was washing breakfast dishes when she heard the front door slam. Her heart began pounding like a trip-hammer.

He stopped short when he came on her in the kitchen. Beard stubble was thick on his face. His clothes were wrinkled. The anguish in his eyes was easily read.

Hawley pride was shredded, but there was enough left to prompt: "Are you full of liquor?"

"Don't talk to me."

"You still feelin' sorry for yourself?"

He turned on his heel. "I'm going to bed."

"Gage! Wait!"

"For what? Another one of your plots designed to separate me from house and money?"

"You didn't have to go off last night. You coulda slept in your own bed. You coulda slept with me. You coulda listened!" She was talking to his back. Phoebe raced into the living room, scooped out her purse from beneath the sofa pillow. He was disrobing when she burst into his room.

"Get out!"

"Look!" She unzipped her purse, dragged out the bills. "This is what I got put by for a place for my folks. I never meant them to stay here. First thing Monday morning, I'm gonna find them a place."

"Good. Include yourself." He kicked off his loafers and lay down on the bed.

"I love you, Gage."

"Sounds glib now. How many men between Cottontown and Bayou La Batre have you told that?"

"None! And you well know it."

"That was probably one of your tricks, too."

Wounded, Phoebe's face flamed. "If I was bigger'n you I'd beat you up for sayin' that."

He turned over, faced the wall. "You're misdirecting the famous Hawley pride. It doesn't affect me one way or another anymore."

Tears of frustration welled up in her eyes. "If I was Velma, I'd go out and drown myself, too!"

He tugged the bedspread up over his head. "Don't let that stop you."

A door slammed. Phoebe went to the window. Her family was back from church. "You can vex me Gage Morgan, but you better not be mean to my folks!" She lifted the bedspread off his face. His eyes were closed, his mouth parted, his breathing soft and regular. Phoebe leaned down and sniffed. He hadn't been drinking.

In her heart she was certain that he hadn't flown into the arms of another woman, either. She was beginning to think sex was a trial to Gage. When they'd stepped from the shower yesterday afternoon his legs wouldn't hold him.

All wasn't lost. She wouldn't let it be. It was a matter of Hawley pride butting heads with Morgan pride. Pride was a good thing. Pride went before a fall. Pride... A sharp dart of misery enclosed her heart. Why hadn't anybody ever told her that pride got in the way of love?

"WE CAN'T STAY?" Annabelle looked from Phoebe to the chicks. They were scratching in the rich sandy loam as Elmo turned up each shovelful.

"I got a business now, Ma. I can help you. There's just too many of us Hawleys for Gage to accept all at once."

"But you said in your letter—"

"I wrote out of turn. And...I may have to move with you."

"Look at Pa," Annabelle said. "Even on his knees he can turn a fair garden."

"Ma, you're not listenin' to me."

"There's room aplenty for us here."

Phoebe shook her head. "It's not the room—"

"You just have to tell your man. I allus told Pa."

"Because you had to. Gage ain't like that. I can't . . . I want to be a Morgan."

"Once a Hawley allus a Hawley."

"You weren't a Hawley before you married Pa."

Annabelle lifted her head. "You're sayin' I misrendered Hawley pride? Ain't it allus got us—"

"I don't want backbone, Ma. I want Gage Morgan."

Phoebe was struggling with a new kind of angle on pride. But the words wouldn't court her tongue, and Ma was steeped in her ways. She could see now that Hawley pride had been conjured up out of thin air.

"You'll give up your family to git him?"

"I'll never give you up. I've got to find a way for us all to fit."

"We ain't goin' back to Vinnie's. She's mean to Pa and Erlene."

Phoebe could see some things about the Hawleys from Vinnie's point of view now. But it wouldn't do to mention it. "You won't have to. There's work in Bayou La Batre. Tomorrow we'll find a place to live and Tuesday I'll take you over to the crab house."

"I don't know nothin' about crabs."

"It's easier than pickin' cotton. I got to cook dinner now. You want to choose somethin' out of the freezer?"

"Lor! I like just standin' there staring into it. Will your man sup with us?"

Gage didn't come out of his room until early the next morning. Phoebe heard him first in the bathroom, then stirring in the kitchen. She waited until she smelled coffee perking to move off the sofa and creep into the bath for her own ablutions. Now that it was short, her hair wasn't so wild. She scrubbed her face, then pinched her cheeks, making them glow beneath her newly acquired tan.

Gage was standing at the sink, staring out the window. The sun was only just beginning to cast a faint light on the horizon.

"We're getting out today," she said.

He turned to face her. Phoebe didn't like the expression he wore. He wasn't giving in. Her shoulders sagged, but out of long habit, she straightened.

"The sooner the better," he said.

"What do I tell Dorie?"

"You don't have to tell her anything."

"What about the crab business? You takin' it back?"

"Have it. Last thing in the world I want is to be accused of starving the Hawley clan. Might ruin my image in the community."

Phoebe almost buckled under his sarcasm. "Are you ever gonna get over bein' mad?"

"What I'm going to get over is you."

"I was wrong. Hidin' my motives from you."

"Makes my heart swell with pride hearing you confess the errors of your ways."

Hawley vainglory may have been conjured out of thin air, but gumption within Phoebe had solidified. It was so hard and thick in her she could taste it. She saw Gage through the haze of recent memory, their love and loving slowly disintegrating, breaking into hundreds of tiny fragments. The kitchen was warm. She was cold and she gambled it all. "I ain't grovelin'. I ain't beggin'." She was holding herself stiffly, her fists clenched. "I ain't beggin' anyone for anything! You don't want me, ever. Say so. Say it plain without soakin' your words in meanness. Just plain up and say goodbye. I won't even speak to you on the street."

"Phoebe!"

The voice came from behind and was filled with panic.

Phoebe didn't take her eyes from Gage. "Go back to bed, Maydean. Now!"

"Erlene's gone."

For a moment everything went out of focus. Phoebe felt scared. But Gage was standing there, looking at her, seemingly holding his breath, his mouth so close to shaping words she didn't dare move.

"I'll help you look for your sister," he said. "If she's slipped outside she could get hurt in the yard."

"Check all the bedrooms, Maydean."

"I already did. And the living room and the bathroom. She ain't in the house. I thought she was in here with you and Gage. That's why—"

Gage went out the door.

Shaking, Phoebe untensed all in a rush. "Go wake Ma and Dorie. They can help us look."

Two hours later the sun was full up and there was still no sign of Erlene.

"She's drowned," wailed Annabelle. "She walked off the land into the water and just kept on walkin' till the water swallowed her up."

Phoebe stroked her mother's arm. "She wouldn't do that, Ma. She don't hardly like to take a bath."

"Erlene wanders off and wanders back," put in Elmo. He crabbed on his walking sticks to the kitchen table and sat down. "In between times, can we eat?"

"Maybe she got snakebit and—"

"Shush that, Willie-Boy." Phoebe glanced up as Gage entered the kitchen. He shook his head.

"I searched the far reaches of the yard. The gate was open—"

"I didn't lock it last night, and you—" Gage had been in his room at dusk. The thought brought all that was unsettled between them rushing back. Steadying herself, she gripped the back of a chair. "That's what she's done. Wandered outside the yard. I'll take the truck—"

"Willie-Boy and I can ride our bikes and look," said Dorie. "We can go down to the point."

"If it's all right with your pa," Phoebe said, watching Gage for his reaction. He nodded. "I'll take all the side roads. We may have to knock on doors. Erlene will follow a cat or dog . . ." Phoebe hated laying out her sister's shortcomings in front of Gage. But Erlene couldn't help being simpleminded.

"I'll start up at the main road and work my way back," he said.

"What about work?"

"It'll keep."

"Did we look under beds?" asked Annabelle distractedly. "I recall that once—"

"We did, Ma. Make some coffee and sandwiches, why don't you?"

Annabelle brightened. "I will. I'll fry bacon. That smell brings Erlene quick as a flea."

"I can't put in no garden on an empty stomach," said Elmo.

Phoebe looked at Gage over the heads of her family. She wondered what he thought of them all, what thoughts he had of her. She wondered most of all what his answer would've been had Maydean not burst in on them. He walked beside her to where their trucks were parked. Phoebe was careful that their arms didn't brush or touch. "I'm sorry about the trouble with Erlene," she said.

"It's not your fault. Or anybody's that I can see. I'll check back about every twenty minutes."

"Erlene's the reason I can't leave Ma and Pa to their own devices," she stated, feeling that her words were assuring her of lifelong separation from him. She couldn't fault him for that. Erlene was a responsibility no man would be willing to take on. And Erlene would need a lookout until the day she died.

Phoebe saw the frown on Gage's brow deepen, saw the pained look he gave her. Words couldn't have said more.

Woeful, she turned away and climbed into her truck. He was never going to forgive her. She'd just have to live with it.

HEARTSICK AND WEARY Phoebe said, "Mayhap now we'll have to call the police." Dorie and Willie-Boy were riding their bikes in circles in front of the junkyard.

Watching them made Phoebe dizzy. She plopped down on the stoop.

"The police might have already picked her up," said Gage. "We should've called them earlier."

Phoebe gave Gage a thankful look. He was being polite, helpful, not taking the anger he held against herself out on her folks.

"The police might send her away!" cried Annabelle.

Phoebe moved to console her mother. "No they wouldn't, I don't think. But sometimes Erlene can't recall she's a Hawley. Why she might be sittin' in the station this very minute havin' herself a high old time. I'll go call. And Ma, why don't you fix some lunch?"

"Won't do no good. Bacon didn't call Erlene in, won't nothin' now."

"I worry better on a full stomach," said Elmo.

Dorie and Willie-Boy came racing up to the porch. "Erlene's comin'!"

Erlene came skipping through the gate, holding the hand of—Phoebe thought her eyes were deceiving her— It was Stout's hand that Erlene was swinging with gay abandon.

"This is my new friend," Erlene said, including everyone in one of her wonderful smiles. "Her name's Marianna." She looked at Stout. "That's right, ain't it?"

Stout's red face blossomed a deeper shade. "That's right, honey."

"I never thought to ask at the crab house," said Phoebe.

"She did just fine," said Stout.

"Fine at what?" chorused Phoebe and Annabelle.

"I learned a new game, didn't I, Marianna. Anybody can play. You get in line, then you have to sit down and the one who fills up the pots first gets money. Look." Erlene held out a handful of bills. "Oh! I lost my quarter. I had a quarter. I have to find my quarter."

Phoebe took hold of Erlene. "I'll send Willie-Boy and Dorie to find it. You just stay here and tell us—"

"Hank put her to work," said Stout. "I picked up right away that she was . . . was . . . she was so eager, I just let her pick. Lord, can she pick. She told Hank she was Erlene Hawley. Hank said he'd put a Hawley to work any day of the week. He says she can work all she wants." Stout appeared suddenly embarrassed. "I'll look after her. It ain't no trouble to me." Her face kept blooming. "I got to get back. My husband'll be by to pick me up any minute."

Erlene started to cry. "Stay and play with me."

"In the morning," Stout said, retrieving her hand, then apropos of nothing she said, "I had me a daughter oncet. Lost her to rheumatic fever when she was six." She patted Erlene on the shoulder. "You be ready at seven o'clock, I'll come get you."

Confused, Erlene pleaded. "I don't know seven o'clock."

"I'll have her ready," said Phoebe. "And, Stout—I mean, Marianna—thank you." They all watched for a moment as the heavyset woman shuffled off. Phoebe sighed. "I see what happened. Erlene saw the pickers waitin' to go to work out in front of the crab house. Her curiosity did the rest." Phoebe handed Erlene's money to Annabelle. "We'll add this to what I already got, Ma. It'll rent us a nice place."

"Imagine! Erlene earnin' money." Annabelle glowed. "Maybe Erlene ain't as loose-minded as we first suspected."

"Maybe not. Maydean, you help Erlene get a bath. I got to get us packed up." Phoebe shot a glance at Gage, but his expression was unreadable. Probably glad he was escaping the Hawleys, she thought. Marry one and you married them all. She could see now, that was asking too much of any man. Her heart wrenched, but she smiled at him anyway.

He didn't smile back.

PHOEBE HELD UP the eyelet-trimmed dress and inspected its lines against her body. She'd pack it last, she decided. That'd make it seem as if she were holding onto her dream—and Gage—a little longer. Her throat was closed up so tightly, she couldn't even cry.

"That's a pretty dress."

Phoebe spun around. Gage closed the door and leaned against it. Phoebe caressed him with her eyes, soaking up his image to take with her. "Guess it don't matter if you see it now. Bad luck was trailin' me afore I ever bought it."

"We have a conversation to finish."

"We don't. I already know what your answer was gonna be. I don't fault you for it. But I take back what I said. I'll speak to you on the street. I appreciate you helpin' look for Erlene. I guess you can tell she's loose-minded."

"No more than me."

Phoebe's head came up. "I never noted any signs—"

Gage laughed softly. "Well, I'd say I'm more along the lines of a horse's ass. I wanted to punish you, make you suffer—"

"You sure did that. I've been about as miserable as a tadpole in a dry hole."

"You *did* con me," he continued. "But the things about you that I like . . . love—your loyalty, your family spirit—that's something no one's ever given to me until you offered it. I like what your love means. You're important to your family. They need you. You're important to me. Dorie, too." He exhaled slowly. "I need you, Phoebe. I don't want to live without you."

Phoebe wasn't sure she was hearing what she was hearing. She was scared to move, scared to breathe. Her heart began to pound. She wanted it to stop so the noise wouldn't distract her.

Her legs were trembling. She sat down on the edge of the bed. "You're not mad at me anymore?"

"I'm furious."

Phoebe's "oh" was scarcely a thread of sound.

"But not so furious and stupid that I want to give up what we had—have. That is, if—?"

It was her backbone, not the limp rags that were her legs, that got her across the room and into his arms. "Gage!"

"Oh, hell. Don't start crying."

"I thought I'd lost you forever." Her hands began to roam, touching, feeling, assuring herself that he was real, solid, that she wasn't wishing so hard she was dreaming his presence.

His hands gripped her shoulders, held her away from him. "No more sly secrets?"

"Nary a one. Ever. Don't hold me away from you. Let me touch you." She reached for him.

"Not there, dammit! There's too many ears in this house."

"One feel?"

"No. Sit over there in the chair. I want to talk to you about your family. While I was driving around looking for Erlene, I had an idea."

"Your tallywhacker's up. I can see it."

"I've lost ten pounds to worry and sex since we met. Do you want a bridegroom who can't keep his pants up during the wedding?"

"Pa'll loan you his suspenders."

Gage's throat constricted. "You're heartless," he said, wavering.

Phoebe reached around him and locked the door. "I just want to show you how much I love you. How much I'll always love you. I don't know any other way to show you. And, anyway," she whispered, "I've been so scared. I've never loved anyone as hard as I love you."

Gage pushed her down on the bed and held her still with his body. "I know. I knew it without you having to say it."

"Just kiss me once, and then you can tell me your idea."

He was utterly unable to resist her. "Once—"

PHOEBE PICKED UP Gage's hand and kissed it. "Don't call me Phoebe or darlin'. Call me Mrs. Morgan. I got to get used to it."

"You have an entire lifetime to get used to it." He sighed and began to loosen his tie. "I'm glad everyone's gone. I thought they'd never leave."

Phoebe laughed. "It was the food. Ma sure can cook. There'd been extra guests at the wedding. On Erlene's account Marianna Stout and her husband had been invited. Phoebe then felt obliged to ask Essie and her husband and Gage had asked Truman Martin to be his best man. The best man's wife was Belle Martin who tried to overkiss the groom. But Phoebe had shot her dagger-looks, besides using her elbow to good advantage.

Phoebe went to the screened door and peered out. Gage's idea had been a mobile home, used but nice, complete with appliances and a built-in air conditioner. Ma was ecstatic.

Gage had hired a crew to clear off a lot and set the trailer up a hundred yards away—hollering distance, but not so close as to mar their own privacy. Not that the distance kept Maydean, Willie-Boy and Dorie from running in and out. But now when Ma came over to the Morgans', she knocked on the door.

Ma was going to work at the crab house with Erlene. And Pa, good at sitting in one spot for hours on end, occupied the cash shack, which freed Gage to concentrate on the welding shop.

Phoebe hugged herself. She didn't think there was a happier woman on the face of the earth.

"While you're standing there, put the latch on that door," said Gage.

Phoebe did his bidding and turned to face him. The length and breadth of him in his wedding suit took her breath away. "You look so handsome."

"You look good enough to eat. Come over here."

Phoebe sat on the sofa, snuggling into his arms. "We ought to take off our good clothes."

He nibbled on her ear. "That's the best suggestion you've made in a week."

She adjusted herself so that she could unbutton his shirt and run her fingertips through the hair on his chest. "It's wonderful being married...wonderful...."

Gage said, "I'm out of my mind with wanting you. I've never been so turned on by anyone in my life. Watching you haul in crabs, hanging out clothes... damn! I kept thinking I'd go out in the boat with you or drag you behind the chicken coop."

"I stayed outta your bed because I didn't want you lookin' peaked when we got married."

Gage raised his head. "Do I look peaked to you?"

Phoebe gave him a slow smile. "Parts of you do."

"Which part is that?"

"It's covered up, but I can feel it just beggin' to get out."

"Let's go in our bedroom and turn it loose."

"I'm never gonna turn it loose."

Gage sagged a little. He'd have to start taking vitamins. One every single day for the rest of his life. He knew it.

"Are you happy?" Phoebe asked. He was already naked, lying propped on pillows.

"I'm unhappy. Happy will be when you get in this bed with me."

Phoebe took her clothes off slowly. Naked, liking the response she was drawing from Gage, she paraded across the room and pulled down the shade. "I told Ma when she saw the shade go up, she could send Dorie home."

"The way I'm feeling that might be a week from now."

She stood at the foot of the bed, eyeing him from head to foot. She crawled up his legs and settled herself upright on the part she liked best. Gage closed his eyes and made a soft guttural sound of pleasure.

"Is it all right if I just sit here a minute?"

His eyes flew open, focused an instant on her face, then on her pert shapely breasts. "No, it's not all right." His insides were beginning to hum, his hips arched.

"Tell me exactly what you're feeling right this second."

"Incredible pain," he whispered. "Move a little bit this way. Yes, that's better. Now a little that way."

A gnawing urgency began working its way up Phoebe's spine. "But, that's doing it!"

"Uh-huh." His lips curled into a lazy grin. "My but you catch on quick." He put his hands on her waist and pulled her down, glorying in the feel of her flesh against his own. Hawley pride and *two* vitamins a day, he thought. He could get through life on that.

Harlequin Temptation

COMING NEXT MONTH

Janet Dailey
Americana

A romantic tour of America with
Janet Dailey!

Enjoy two releases each month from this
collection of your favorite previously
published Janet Dailey titles, presented
alphabetically state by state.

Available NOW wherever paperback books
are sold.

Harlequin Intrigue

In October
Watch for the new look of

Harlequin Intrigue
...because romance can be quite an adventure!

Each time, Harlequin Intrigue brings you great stories, mixing a contemporary, sophisticated romance with the surprising twists and turns of a puzzler...romance with "something more."

Plus...
in next month's publications of Harlequin Intrigue we offer you the chance to win one of four mysterious and exciting weekends. Don't miss the opportunity! Read the October Harlequin Intrigues!

For the millions who can't read
Give the Gift of Literacy

One out of five adults in North America
cannot read or write well enough
to fill out a job application
or understand the directions on a bottle of medicine.

**You can change all this by joining the fight
against illiteracy.**

For more information write to:
Contact, Box 81826, Lincoln, Neb. 68501
In the United States, call toll free: 1-800-228-8813

**The only degree you need
is a degree of caring**

LIT-A-1R